Scouts

JIMMY Patterson Books for Young Readers

James Patterson Presents
Ernestine, Catastrophe Queen by Merrill Wyatt
How to Be a Supervillain by Michael Fry
How to Be a Supervillain: Born to Be Good by Michael Fry
How to Be a Supervillain: Bad Guys Finish First by Michael Fry
The Unflushables by Ron Bates
Sci-Fi Junior High by John Martin and Scott Seegert
Sci-Fi Junior High: Crash Landing by John Martin and Scott Seegert

The Middle School Series by James Patterson
Middle School, The Worst Years of My Life
Middle School: Get Me Out of Here!
Middle School: Big Fat Liar
Middle School: How I Survived Bullies, Broccoli, and Snake Hill
Middle School: Ultimate Showdown
Middle School: Save Rafe!
Middle School: Just My Rotten Luck
Middle School: Dog's Best Friend
Middle School: Escape to Australia
Middle School: From Hero to Zero
Middle School: Born to Rock

The I Funny Series by James Patterson
I Funny
I Even Funnier
I Totally Funniest
I Funny TV
I Funny: School of Laughs
The Nerdiest, Wimpiest, Dorkiest I Funny Ever

The Treasure Hunters Series by James Patterson
Treasure Hunters
Treasure Hunters: Danger Down the Nile
Treasure Hunters: Secret of the Forbidden City
Treasure Hunters: Peril at the Top of the World
Treasure Hunters: Quest for the City of Gold
Treasure Hunters: All-American Adventure

The House of Robots Series by James Patterson
House of Robots
House of Robots: Robots Go Wild!
House of Robots: Robot Revolution

The Daniel X Series by James Patterson
The Dangerous Days of Daniel X
Daniel X: Watch the Skies
Daniel X: Demons and Druids
Daniel X: Game Over
Daniel X: Armageddon
Daniel X: Lights Out

Other Illustrated Novels and Stories
Max Einstein: The Genius Experiment
Dog Diaries
Katt vs. Dogg
Unbelievably Boring Bart
Not So Normal Norbert
Laugh Out Loud
Pottymouth and Stoopid
Jacky Ha-Ha
Jacky Ha-Ha: My Life Is a Joke
Public School Superhero
Word of Mouse
Give Please a Chance
Give Thank You a Try
Big Words for Little Geniuses
Cuddly Critters for Little Geniuses
The Candies Save Christmas

For exclusives, trailers, and other information, visit jimmypatterson.org.

Scouts

SHANNON GREENLAND

Foreword by James Patterson

JIMMY Patterson Books
Little, Brown and Company
New York Boston London

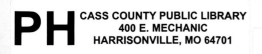

Copyright © 2019 by Shannon Greenland
Foreword © 2019 by James Patterson

JIMMY Patterson Books / Little, Brown and Company
Hachette Book Group
1290 Avenue of the Americas, New York, NY 10104
JimmyPatterson.org

First Edition: July 2019

JIMMY Patterson Books is an imprint of Little, Brown and Company, a
division of Hachette Book Group, Inc. The Little, Brown name and logo
are trademarks of Hachette Book Group, Inc. The JIMMY Patterson
Books® name and logo are trademarks of JBP Business, LLC.

Cataloging-in-publication data is available at the Library of Congress.

ISBN (hc) 978-0-316-52478-0

10 9 8 7 6 5 4 3 2 1

LSC-C

Printed in the United States of America

For my parents, who made my childhood full of fun and adventure.

FOREWORD

Best friends are the ones who share your deepest secrets, complain with you about school, laugh with you so hard your belly hurts, and go on epic adventures with you, sometimes without even leaving the house. Your friends understand you in a special way because they're going through a lot of the same things that you are, and they know you almost as well as you know yourself. I've had some of my friends for a long, long time, and even though we don't see each other every day, our bonds are still strong and always will be.

Scouts is a wonderful story about good friends who nevertheless might be on the edge of drifting apart. Growing up and having different interests can sometimes do that. One night, they decide to go on a seemingly simple trek to check out a crashed meteor, but instead they find danger, thrills, heartbreak, and joy...and discover just how deep their friendships really go.

Everyone needs friends like the Scouts, and after reading this story, I hope you'll feel like they're your friends as well.

—James Patterson

Scouts

CHAPTER 1

1985 — The Here and Now

The walkie-talkie crackles on my bedroom desk. "Annie, come in. Beans here."

I snatch up the gadget. "This is Annie. Over."

"Don't forget your walkie. Over."

I roll my eyes. So typical of Beans. Like I would ever forget my walkie. "Yeah. Over."

Unzipping my backpack, I start cramming in all the stuff I'll need for our camping trip: ball cap and toothbrush (I hate dirty teeth), chore money (last time I counted, I had twenty-three dollars and thirteen cents), box of matches, flashlight, can of Pringles, and I finish it all up with my sleeping bag.

I'm digging under my bed for some spare batteries when Mom peeks in my open door. "Annie, do you want to take... is that your new yellow dress *crumpled* on the floor?"

I look out from under my bed and cringe. Whoops.

With a sigh, she sits down on my bed. "What am I going to do with you, Annie? Your room is a disaster."

"I'll clean up when I come home. Promise." Standing, I give her my best smile because I so don't have time to clean up right now. The Scouts are waiting.

Mom looks me up and down for a second, taking in my cutoffs and Guns N' Roses tee, before letting out another sigh. Uh-oh.

"I think we need to talk." She pats the spot next to her on the bed. "Sit down for a second."

My shoulders drop. "What? Why? Am I in trouble?"

"No," she says. "It's just... it's just... well—"

I hold my breath. What's going on?

"You're getting older now. You're not a little girl anymore. Your friends aren't little boys, either. Before too much longer, those boys are going to want to do different things and they might not want you to come along. You're going to want to do different things, too."

"What? No!" I snap, knowing that's never going to happen. "They're my only friends!"

"I know." Mom runs her fingers down one of my

two dark braids. "But maybe it's time you made some friends who are girls."

Dad sticks his head in the open door, just back from work and still wearing his suit and tie. "My goodness, you two look so alike."

Everyone always says that, and it's true. Mom's Native American genes definitely dominated over Dad's Caucasian ones. But it's especially true right now because we're both wearing our hair in braids with bandanas. Me because it's what I always do, and Mom because she's been painting our kitchen.

My mom gives my dad a look. "Honey, I was just telling Annie that we think she should start making some friends who are girls."

Dad looks confused for a second. "Oh, yeah. Right." His gaze takes in my stuffed backpack. "I didn't realize you were camping out with the Scouts tonight."

I nod. I love when he uses our club name, even if we're not real Scouts.

"Where're you going to be?"

"Rocky's."

He gives me a warning look. "Stay at Rocky's. Do not go anywhere else."

I nod again so I don't have to answer him. I'm more

of a lie-by-omission type of person. When it comes to actually speaking a lie, I stink at it. Now, Fynn—he's the good liar in our group. He can open his mouth and tell you whatever you want to hear, and you'll believe it. Yeah, that'd be a good skill to have.

Dad looks at my overstuffed backpack again. "I'm serious, Annie. Only Rocky's. No wandering off."

"How was work today?" I ask him.

Dad points his finger at me. "Do not go on Mr. Basinger's farm. And definitely do *not* climb up his silo again!"

I nod again. So much for changing the subject.

Sure, Old Man Basinger hasn't exactly warmed up to us Scouts yet—he yells at us, rides his tractor waving a shotgun, even threw a peach at us once—but we know how to skirt around him.

I look between my parents. "Can I go now?"

Dad's lips tilt up into a little smile. "Not before I give you something." He reaches into his pocket and pulls out a small object. "Hold out your hand."

I don't hide the giant smile that creeps onto my cheeks as I bounce off the bed and hurry over. Dad always gives the best presents. I hold out my hand and watch as he opens his.

A purple pocketknife drops into my palm!

My eyes widen. "For real?" I can't believe Mom agreed to this.

"I think you're old enough."

I stand up a little taller. I can't wait to show the Scouts!

Dad chuckles. "Okay. Go. Have fun."

"But we're not done talking about the boy/girl stuff," Mom says. "We'll finish up later. Just think about what I said."

I definitely will not be thinking about it, but I nod anyway as I grab my pack and walkie-talkie, yell, "Love you!" and fly downstairs. I climb onto the BMX bike that Dad and I built last summer and hit the street, taking off toward Rocky's house.

Rocky's dad's Trans Am is up on blocks, as it always is. Sometimes he lets me crawl under and help him with stuff. He's cool that way. I wish my dad could do stuff like work on cars. All he does is wear a suit and go to an office.

Though he did help me build my bike, so there is that.

Rocky's sister is shooting hoops outside their garage when I pedal up. Everybody in his family is an athlete, which is why I love hanging out over here. One of them is always up for playing basketball, catch, football, or soccer.

His dad played football for UT, and Rocky's been playing forever, too. A lot of people in the neighborhood say Rocky's got raw talent and could go pro someday. That'd be neat—having a superstar friend and all.

Rocky's already outside waiting on his bike, dressed in his usual jeans and muscle tee. He catches a wheelie off the ramp we all built in his side yard and meets up with me on the street.

"You are such a girl," he jokingly complains.

"I can do anything you can do, and better, so what exactly are you getting at?"

"Hello?" He holds up his wrist, which doesn't have a watch. "I've been waiting forever."

"Um, let me remind you that Fynn is typically the one we're waiting on, so that has nothing to do with being a girl. Besides, my parents wanted to talk."

"About what?"

I feel my cheeks heat as I think back to the conversation. "Nothing," I say, pedaling off. "Let's just go."

We hang a left and come up on Beans's house, and Rocky and I brake to a stop in front and wait.

A couple of seconds go by, and then Beans opens the door and steps out. His mom follows right behind him, sticking her finger in his face and saying something. I listen real close and make out "B minus" and "no more TV" and "your father's going to be very disappointed."

Beans is a straight-A student. I'm sure a B minus to his mom is like a D to mine.

I watch as Beans stands in his high-water jeans, staring down at the porch, and my chest aches. I hate what he must be feeling. I don't know why his mom is always railing on him. And I don't know why she doesn't buy him clothes that fit. I mean, they're the richest family in the neighborhood.

She finishes whatever she's saying and then turns to look across their front yard at me and Rocky. She straightens up and gives us a big wave, like she wasn't just all up in Beans's face. "Y'all kids be good."

"We will," we say, and watch as Beans climbs onto his bike and quietly pedals the length of his driveway to meet us.

When Beans's mom closes the door, he immediately ruffles his Afro to rub out the side-part that she always puts there.

"Everything okay?" I ask.

"Fine," he snaps, and then does this thing where he peels his lips off his braces before racing off.

9

He's been snapping a lot lately.

"Beans's mom is so strict," I whisper to Rocky.

"I know," he says. "Let's just go."

We hurry to catch him, pedaling furiously up the hill, and squeal to a stop in front of Fynn's house. There's a new car in front. A Buick. Sounds from the backyard filter around.

"I'll just stay here," Rocky says.

"What?" I drop my bike. "Why? Come on."

With a sigh, Rocky gets off his bike and slowly follows me and Beans. As we round the corner of Fynn's house, we see everyone sitting on Fynn's deck, finishing dinner and laughing. Fynn's mom, another woman who looks just like his mom, and a girl about our age. With all their blond hair and preppy clothes, they look like a staged magazine ad.

And here's me with my bandana, Beans in his highwaters, and Rocky with his muscle tee, looking like a bunch of hoodlums (to use Mom's word) leaning up against the fence that surrounds their backyard.

"Hello, son."

I turn to see Rocky's dad coming out the back door of Fynn's house, and my head snaps over to Rocky.

Rocky mumbles hello but totally avoids eye contact with me. And before I can ask him what the deal is, Fynn comes off the deck toward us, high-fiving Rocky's dad as he passes.

When Fynn's standing right in front of us, I look between my two friends. "Anybody going to tell me what's going on?"

Fynn furrows his brows. "With what?"

"Hello?" I wave my hand in the direction of the back door. "Rocky's dad?"

Fynn looks at Rocky. "I thought you told them."

Rocky shrugs but still doesn't say anything. I glance over at Beans, and he looks as clueless as me.

"His dad and my mom are dating," Fynn tells us with a smile that so doesn't match Rocky's attitude.

"That's kind of neat," Beans says. "If they get married, you two will be brothers."

Fynn nods. "Cool, huh?"

I look over at Rocky. "How long?"

"Couple weeks," he mumbles.

I want to be irritated he didn't tell me, but clearly there's something going on. Rocky's mom died several years ago, and he doesn't talk much about it, but I suspect this right here has got to stink. I think about my own parents, and yeah, it would totally bum me out if one of them died and the other started dating someone.

But at least it's Fynn's mom, who is usually really nice and not strict like Beans's mom.

The laughter from the deck filters over again, and the girl who was sitting beside Fynn gets up and comes bounding over, blond curls bouncing.

"Wow," I hear Beans breathe, and I cut him a look right as Rocky must spot her, too, because he straightens up from the fence.

Wide-eyed, both Beans and Rocky stare as she comes toward us—tank top, miniskirt, bow in her hair, and ankle socks. It reminds me of those Pert shampoo commercials where there's obviously a fan off-camera blowing the girl's hair. This is exactly how Mom would have me dress if she could get her way. The "perfect" girl.

Well, there are a lot of "perfect" girls at school who are also perfectly mean. I don't get it—what's so great about being pretty?

"Hi." The girl grins, all dimples and lip gloss and freckles. "I'm Scarlett, Fynn's cousin."

"Hi!" Beans squeaks, and then clears his throat.

"Hey." Rocky pitches his voice low, and I roll my eyes.

Fynn pulls a tissue from his back pocket and blows his nose. "Scarlett lives in Chicago. She's going into the eighth grade. She's here for the week while her mom goes off and gets married."

Wait a minute, "for the week"? I hope that doesn't mean what I think it means.

"Are you going to come watch the meteor shower with us?" Beans asks, and I shoot him the evil eye. This was supposed to be our secret adventure night! Just the Scouts.

She nods. "Fynn says we're camping out, too. Let me just get my purse."

Her *purse*?

She races inside, and I watch as her miniskirt bounces with each step. We're supposed to be climbing a silo. I hope she's changing.

"What are you doing?" I grumble at Fynn. "Why did you invite her?"

He refolds his tissue into a neat square. "My mom said I had to bring her along."

"But this is our first-day-of-summer camping trip. We do it every year. *Just. Us*," I emphatically point out. What's wrong with him?

Fynn just shrugs. "Sorry. Mom said."

"She's a girl," Rocky whispers.

I frown. "I'm a girl."

"Yeah, but she's a real girl. A woman."

A *woman*? She's going into the eighth grade!

"She's going to be here the whole week?" Rocky asks with so much wonder in his tone that I start chewing my thumbnail.

"Yeah." Fynn sighs, all put-out, and walks his used tissue over to the garbage.

Well, at least I'm not the only one none too thrilled with her arrival and intrusion on our week.

CHAPTER 2

Scarlett's bike has pink and purple tassels, a white basket, and an annoying horn—and she can't keep up. Me and Beans take off to Basinger's farm, leaving Rocky and Fynn back with her. They know where we're going. They'll catch up.

At least Scarlett put on some pants. Even if they are neon-pink spandex. Now she won't flash everyone with her undies when she's climbing the silo.

We drop our bikes, tucking them under our usual hiding tree, and we take a second to survey Basinger's land. I honestly don't know where it starts and stops; there's so much of it. It's a dairy farm with two barns, lots of cows, hay fields, and a few houses scattered around, where Mr. Basinger's sons and their families live.

The good thing about the silo we plan on climbing is that it's an old one they don't use anymore, and it sits in a back pasture, pretty much out of view. It's also the tallest thing in the area. Perfect for stargazing.

On the way here, I tried to ask Beans about what went down with his mom, but he just gave me a snippy "Nothing." But Beans tells me things he doesn't tell the others, and so before Fynn and Rocky catch up, I try one last time. "Hey, anything you want to talk about? You know I'll keep it between us."

He looks away, and a beat or two goes by, and I'm totally expecting another "Nothing." But then he shakes his head and turns to me, and slowly, his dark eyes fill with tears. The sight unnerves me. I've never seen him cry, not even when that bully on the bus punched him.

"Beans?" I hesitantly ask.

"We're losing our house," he quietly admits. "And I might have to go live with my dad."

"I don't understand."

"It's being foreclosed on. Mom says Dad didn't give her enough alimony and child support, but Dad says she spent all the money on herself instead of paying the bills." Beans sniffs and wipes his nose with the back of his hand. "I don't know. They went to court and everything."

I think about the way his mom dresses and the fancy car she drives. Their house, too. Super nice with the big pool in back, where we always hang out. "But I thought you were rich?"

Beans just shakes his head, and I reach over and give him a hug as my mind starts to reel with memories. . . .

Rigging his room with fishing line to catch the tooth fairy. Camping out in his living room with a Scooby-Doo sheet for a tent. Cooking chili dogs with his mom's curling iron.

This can't be happening. Beans can't leave. He's one of my best friends.

Maybe he can come live with me. Or maybe we can convince his mom to sell her fancy car and pay their bills.

"We'll figure it out," I tell him.

"I know all y'all think my mom is mean, but really she's just stressed."

"We don't think she's mean," I assure him, though of course we do. But I guess her behavior makes sense. She might be losing everything, including Beans.

He smiles weakly. "Don't tell the others yet, okay? I don't want them to know."

If he's embarrassed his mom spent all their money, he doesn't need to be. But I don't say that and instead assure him. "Okay, I won't."

"Promise?"

I give him another quick hug. "I promise."

The others still haven't caught up yet, I'm sure because of Scarlett. So together Beans and I climb through the barbed wire and make our way up the grassy hill toward the silo. Heaven help us if Old Man Basinger ever does one of those fancy electric fences around here. Though Beans could probably figure it out. Some sort of antielectric thingamajig.

I love Beans's inventions. Last year he made a vest that's sort of like one of those Swiss Army knives. Each pocket and zipper and flap doubled as a survival device, but the zipper was the best part. If you removed it, it could be used as a flexible blade to saw wood. Yeah, Beans has got a cool brain. He definitely can't leave. We need him.

I need him.

It's almost dark now, but we don't dare switch on

our flashlights as we approach the silo. I glance back to see Fynn, Rocky, and Scarlett just now dropping their bikes and climbing through the barbed wire. Rocky steps on the bottom strip and pulls the top one up for Scarlett to safely climb through.

He's never held the barbed wire for me. None of them have.

Grabbing on to the first rung of the silo ladder, Beans starts climbing, and I follow behind. Halfway up I stop and look down to see the other three beginning their ascent. Scarlett's babbling and giggling about something, and somewhere in the mix I hear Rocky chuckle. But it's not a real laugh, it's a fake one. He's my friend, and I know the difference.

Frankly, I don't know why people fake-laugh. It's the stupidest thing ever. If I don't think something's funny, I don't laugh. Kind of a no-brainer.

Beans keeps climbing and I follow, and when we reach the top, we crawl under the railing and scooch over to make room for the others. A few minutes later Fynn pops up, followed by Scarlett, and then Rocky.

When they're all on this side of the railing, Scarlett stands for a second and looks out over Basinger's farm. "Wow!" she exclaims, and claps her hands.

Yep, it is pretty impressive.

We lived in Los Angeles before we moved here. I don't remember much, but I do remember a lot of concrete and small houses with even smaller yards. Here it's all green and hilly with trees and fields and mountains in the distance. Mom says it's picturesque.

All I know is that it's just about the best place ever to play and get lost with my friends. Oh, and snow tubing is awesome. Especially when you hit a bump and go flying out of the tube.

I never want to leave. I never want my friends to leave, either.

"Be careful," Rocky tells Scarlett, and motions for her to sit.

Yeah, we wouldn't want her to fall over the railing or anything.

Rocky nudges in to sit between me and Scarlett. Good. I don't want to sit next to her anyway.

"You're wearing a bra," Rocky notices, looking straight at the front of my tee.

Beans giggles. I feel my cheeks get hot as I look down at my white Guns N' Roses tee, and sure enough, I can see the outline of the training bra Mom made me put on. I never get embarrassed, but right now my face goes from red to full-on fire.

I defend myself. "It's a sports thing!"

"That doesn't even make sense," Rocky says.

"Yes, it does." Fynn points to my T-shirt. "Your sister wears one of those when she plays basketball."

Rocky thinks about that a second. "Oh, yeah, true."

"Oh, my God!" I yell. "Can we drop it?"

"What's the big deal?" Scarlett asks. "She's a girl. Girls wear bras."

"But she's Annie," Rocky says. Like that even makes sense. Have the guys really not noticed until now?

"Just shut up," I snap, and then I shove Rocky, sending him right into Scarlett.

She screams, like she's about to plummet to her death, and Rocky grabs her. "I've got you," he says, and she giggles again, and the bra topic is officially over.

Thank God.

Fynn swats his neck. "Great. Mosquitoes." He slides a small spray bottle from his front pocket and squirts it and then offers it to us, but we all shake our heads. He lies back then, and for a few minutes we quietly stare up at the sky and the millions of stars.

Then Beans sits up and rifles around in his bag and pulls out the plastic baby bottle telescope. Rocky and Fynn don't really care about Beans's inventions, but I do, especially when I get to help him make stuff.

This one we made last week in anticipation of the meteor shower. On the small end we wrapped electrical tape around a tiny magnifying glass. We cut the bottom off the larger end of the bottle and taped a bigger magnifier there.

Holding the small end up to his eye, Beans peers through, and eagerly I watch, itching for my turn.

After a few seconds, he hands over the telescope, and I close one eye as I peer through, too. Wow, it really does work. I can see the haloes of light around the stars and everything.

"I made a telescope once," Scarlett says. "It won a National Science Award. The judges said it was the best they had ever seen. There was even this guy there from NASA who took it back with him."

"NASA? Really?" Beans asks, and I think he just fell in love with her brain.

She nods. "Swear to God."

Fynn glances over at me and whispers, "She tells a lot of 'tall tales.'"

I laugh a little, and Fynn reaches for the telescope. "My turn."

I hand the homemade telescope over and then close my eyes and settle back onto the silo. A warm breeze floats past, and I inhale the relaxing scent of grass and hay.

None of us speak for a few moments. If I could freeze time, this would be a good moment right here.

I don't know why my mom was harping on me to make new friends. I know the Scouts are going to be friends forever. I smile a little as I remember the very first time we got into trouble....

Planting his hands on his hips, the principal bent over and got right in our faces. He looked first at me, then Fynn, Rocky, and Beans, then right back at me. "What do you have to say for yourselves?"

I bit my pinky nail. "Dad said carpet that had boric acid on it is fire retarded."

"Retardant," Beans corrected me, and the principal shot him a look.

"So you all just decided to light the hallway carpet on fire and see?" The principal swerved his gaze back to me. "The idea occurred to you all at the same time?"

The Scouts and I exchanged looks. All for one and all that, right? So in perfect synchronicity, we answered, "Yes, sir!"

I knew then I had found my people. I'm about to remind them of that story, when Scarlett's voice breaks the silence. "When's this meteor shower supposed to happen?"

"Any time now," Beans answers.

I hear something pop, and open my eyes. Rocky takes a slurp of RC Cola and passes the can. I take a gulp and burp. Then Beans. Fynn wipes the opening before his own slurp and burp. Then we look at Rocky, who slurped but didn't burp. It's what we do. Gulp RC and burp. Why isn't he burping?

Rocky cuts us a guilty cringe as he swerves his gaze to Scarlett, who is staring at the sky. I narrow my eyes. What, now he's suddenly a gentleman?

"There it is!" Scarlett shouts, and I nearly choke on my next gulp.

Beans scrambles to grab the homemade telescope, and I glance up to the sky to see a single shooting star.

"Cool," Rocky says.

"Yeah," I agree as another streaks across.

Then another. And another.

"Amazing," Fynn says.

"You seeing this?" I ask Beans, and he excitedly nods.

Another. And another. Silently, we all watch as

what seems like dozens of stars streak through the sky. I don't blink. I don't breathe. I don't want to miss anything.

"Oh, my God." Beans points behind us. "Look at that one!"

I swerve around and stare at what starts out as a small white glow trailing through the sky, and I watch as it gets bigger. Bigger. Bigger. This one is going to be way closer than any of the others. I feel the silo begin to vibrate as I realize this shooting star is low. Too low. My heart jumps to my throat. It's—

"It's coming right toward us!" Fynn screams.

Frantically, we scramble over one another, hollering, trying to get down, but it keeps coming. Faster. Faster. Bigger. Bigger. Hissing now. Shaking the air around us.

"Duck!" Rocky yells, and we flatten ourselves to the silo.

Panting, trembling, I stare straight at it, my eyes glued wide, my ears ringing, terror prickling across my skin.

It's going to hit us! Please, God, don't let me die!

An intense bright light flares as the meteor whistles through the air right over our heads.

The silo shakes hard, and the light flashes to

orange, then yellow, and then disappears into the horizon.

And then nothing but silence.

I stay pressed against the silo with my shoulders planted into the warm concrete. Beside me, Fynn gasps, and I know he's about to have an asthma attack.

With a swallow, I push myself up, and with shaky hands, I slide his inhaler from his front pocket and press it into his palm.

Rocky sits up next and looks over at me with a wigged-out expression that I know I must share, too.

"Holy..." Beans whispers.

Together we stare out into the night and miles away to where the meteor fell. A faint yellow glow gradually fades until the whole area blankets to darkness again.

"I bet it's"—Fynn wheezes—"an extraterrestrial."

"Did you watch *Alien* again?" Beans asks.

Fynn sits up on another wheeze. "Maybe."

Rocky agrees. "A UFO, and they're going to suck our brains right out of our heads."

"Only one way we're going to find out." I stand up and look down at all my friends—and Scarlett— and an idea forms. "Scouts, we—"

"Why do you call yourselves Scouts?" she interrupts.

I switch my gaze over to her. "Because our town is too small for an actual Boy Scout troop, so we made our own."

"But you're not a boy," she says.

I ignore her, because that's so not the point, and turn back to my friends. "We are hiking to where that thing went down and we're finding it. This will be our greatest adventure yet." I make sure to look directly at Beans as I say the next part. "I bet whoever finds that meteor will be famous. They'll probably get some kind of major science award and lots of money."

Rocky agrees. "Probably like a million dollars."

I keep looking at Beans. "Think about what we could do with that money."

He nods, clearly now seeing what I am suggesting. "Yeah."

"This will be so much fun!" Scarlett claps her hands.

Oh, heck, no. She's not coming. "It'll be dirty."

She gets up. "So?"

"And also scary. Very, very"—I lean forward— "*very* scary."

"I'm coming with you," she says.

Fynn shakes his head. "No, you're not."

"I'll tell all your parents if you don't let me." Her blond eyebrows knowingly lift.

Collectively we sigh. She has us there.

I fold my arms. "Okay, but this is how it works. We've perfected this over the years, so don't screw it up. We'll set up our campsite in the usual place and leave a note saying we went to the tree house, which is located in Rocky's backyard. In the tree house, we leave a note saying we went to the fort, which we built in that empty lot across from my house. At the fort, we leave a note saying we're in Fynn's basement. By the time they track all the notes, which they never do, we're back from our adventure." This time *I* lift my brows. "Got it?"

She purses her lips. "They never come looking for you?"

"Believe me, we know what we're doing." I look at the Scouts to back me up on this, and they all nod. "Got it?" I ask her again.

She smiles. "Got it."

We all climb down the silo, and as soon as we're back on the grass, Rocky says, "I'll take Scarlett with me to set up the tent, and you guys can do the notes."

"I'll go with you." Fynn starts to follow.

Rocky stops him. "Why don't you leave the notes instead?"

"Oh." Fynn frowns. "Okay, I guess."

They head off in different directions, and I watch Fynn and Rocky for a second. Maybe this trip will be good for them. Or rather, good for Rocky. Maybe it'll help him get over whatever his problem is with their parents dating.

I turn to Beans, who is staring at the purple bandana wrapped around my head. He reaches up and brushes his hand across the top and brings his fingers down to show me some silver glittery stuff.

It's then that I notice the stuff is in his hair, too, and a little bit on our clothes. "What is it?" I ask.

He runs his thumb across the pads of his fingers. "Must be paint from the silo."

I look at Beans for a second, and it really hits me how much he means to me. How truly sad I would be to lose him.

"What?" he asks, picking up on my mood.

"Nothing." I smile. "Beans, if we find that thing, it'll probably be worth a lot of money." Excitement bubbles through me. "You guys can pay your bills, and you won't have to move."

This is huge. Beans can stay right at home where he belongs... with us.

The Scouts.

He brushes his fingers off on his jeans before giving me a huge grin. "I know. Let's go!"

CHAPTER 3

In less than half an hour, everyone is back.

Beans unfolds a map and lays it out on the grass.

"Where'd you get that?" Fynn asks.

Beans peels his lips off his braces. "I snuck back in my house and grabbed it." He flicks on his flashlight, and we all move in to get a closer look. Clicking a mechanical pencil, he makes an X. "This is where we are." He makes another X. "This is where I believe the unknown object went down."

My gaze moves between both Xs. Seems like a long way. "How do you know?"

"Distance equals velocity times time. But I've also factored in the positioning of the moon and the height of the silo. The speed I estimate the object was traveling and my trajectory of—"

"Yeah, yeah, yeah." We all wave our hands in the air. Beans tends to rattle on.

"I believe the meteor is fifteen miles from here." Beans trails his flashlight over the map. "Bikes stay here. We're on foot. I highly doubt we'll be on Basinger's property the whole way. Though if I had time to pull property maps, I'd know for sure." He takes out a compass. "That's a north-by-northwest route."

"Okay, and what about the Mason Mountain Clan?" Fynn gives us all a worried glance. "Anybody thought about them?"

Beans scoffs. "Don't tell me you actually believe those rumors."

Fynn looks at me. I look at Rocky. And we all nervously shrug.

"Sort of," I say.

"Mountain Clan?" Scarlett asks.

"It's nothing," Beans says. "I mean, seriously. Have any of you actually seen one of these Masons?"

We look at one another. Well, no, but still.

Beans nods his head toward the dark mountains emerging from the moonlit horizon. "They're supposed to live up in there somewhere," he tells Scarlett. "Moonshiners. Mean. They kill and eat kids."

Scarlett doesn't say anything for a second, and I think she might suggest we turn back. Which wouldn't be a bad idea—the her-turning-back thing. At least then I'd be rid of her. But she bursts out laughing instead. "What? Like in 'Hansel and Gretel'? You guys have got to be kidding me."

I scowl. I don't like her making fun of us. But put like that, it does sound kind of ridiculous.

"See?" Beans says. "I told you. All the parents tell the kids that story so we won't wander off. I can't believe you guys seriously believe it."

"I didn't say I believed it," Rocky defends himself, and I shoot him an incredulous look. He does too believe it.

Beans turns his flashlight off. "Okay, enough about them. All lights off. We don't want anyone to see us heading out. The moon is bright enough—we can navigate by it and save our batteries."

He climbs through the barbed wire fence, and we follow. Beans can calculate whatever formula he wants. As long as we head in the direction where we saw the thing go down, that's all that matters to me.

We pass the silo and start down the hill toward a thick clump of trees. Way off to the right sits one of Basinger's sons' homes. In the night it twinkles with interior and exterior lights.

In my peripheral vision I see Scarlett slip her backpack off and rub at her shoulders. We've been walking only a few minutes. Really, now? As if on cue, Rocky snatches the backpack from her fingers and starts carrying it. She just grins, and I swear I see him flex his biceps.

She starts to speak and we simultaneously shush her. Not until we get to the trees do we talk. A few minutes later we step into the woods, and Scarlett whispers, "Can I talk now?"

No.

"Yes," Rocky says.

"So what'd you pack?" Scarlett asks me.

I shrug. "The usual. Matches. Pringles. Oh, that's right—I forgot to show y'all my pocketknife!"

I slip it out of the back pocket of my cutoffs and pass it to Beans first, and then it goes to Fynn, then Rocky—all of them clicking it open and checking it out and oohing and aahing. It goes to Scarlett last and she doesn't even look at it as she passes it right back to me.

"I packed underwear," she tells everyone. "Because Mom always says a girl should have extra underwear. I also packed toilet paper so I don't have to wipe with a leaf. And I packed a change of clothes in case I get dirty."

I cut her a sideways look. *Toilet paper?*

"Underwear." Beans nods. "My mom says the same thing."

"So what'd you pack?" she asks Fynn.

"My allergy pills," Fynn answers. "Ointment if I get itchy. BC Powder for my migraines. Drops for my eyes. Neosporin for cuts. Oh, and Band-Aids."

He didn't mention the cookies we made a few days ago. He sure better have brought those.

"Band-Aids." Scarlett nods. "That's a good idea."

She goes on to Rocky next, and I wonder if she's talking just to hear her voice. There's this girl at school who does that. Talks constantly. Drives me nuts. I was complaining about it to Mom one day, and she said some people talk a lot because they like the attention. I think Scarlett might be one of those people. Actually, Fynn's kind of like that, too. Maybe it runs in their family.

"I went on a camping trip with Bryan Right once," she tells us.

"The singer?" I ask. That guy is super famous. He even has his own TV show.

"Yeah. He was so awesome. My dad is his manager. Bryan wanted to take me on a date, but my dad was like, 'No way.'"

"Does your dad go on tour with him?" Beans asks.

"Totally," she says. "Next year he's taking me on the road, too."

I glance over at Fynn to see if she's telling the truth, and he nods.

Wow, a dad who manages Bryan Right. That's got to be about the coolest thing I've ever heard. But there's no way I'll admit that out loud.

"So, what's your dad do?" Scarlett asks Rocky.

"He works at a paper mill. He's a weld—"

"Oh"—she cuts in—"and by the way, I think your dad and Aunt Colleen make the cutest couple ever. I totally saw them kissing earlier."

I look over at Rocky to see the muscles in his jaw tighten up.

Scarlett prattles on. "I hope they get married. I already asked Aunt Colleen if I could be a bridesmaid, and she told me she'd think about it."

They've been dating only a couple of weeks. Aren't people supposed to date longer than that before they start talking marriage? I look at Fynn to see how he's taking this whole thing, and he's just walking along. I wonder if he even realizes Rocky's not happy about this.

I think about the high five Fynn and Rocky's dad shared and about the smile on Fynn's face when he told us the news. Fynn's an only child and he sees his dad, like, once or twice a year. So, yeah, I guess I get it. He probably would be happy about this. Maybe Rocky just doesn't want to share his dad.

Scarlett changes the subject to shopping, then changes the subject again to something about a squirrel bite and rabies shots, and on it continues until I'm nearly ready to yank the bandana off my head and shove it into her mouth.

Eventually, I just tune her out.

Midnight finally rolls around, and before I see it, I hear it.

The river.

And from the rumble and roar, I know we're at the Class V section.

Great.

Just great.

CHAPTER 4

Side by side we stand, looking down into the moonlit river as it churns and crashes over boulders. We all glance up the river. Then down. Then to the other side. That has to be at least twenty feet across.

"Why do we have to be in the rapids section?" I grumble.

Fynn gives me a nudge. "Rocky brought rope. We'll pull you across if we have to."

"Why?" Scarlett asks. "Are you afraid of water?"

Yes. I don't tell her that, though. Of course Rocky decides to volunteer the information. "Annie almost drowned when we were six. My sister saved her."

"I saved someone once," Scarlett starts in, and I promptly tune her out as I stare down at the water.

Maybe we can walk the length of the river until we find a narrower place to cross.

Beans throws his stuff down. "It's too dark. Let's camp here. We'll find a place to cross in the morning."

Rocky tosses his stuff down, too. "Good idea. Plus, I'm hungry."

"Me, too," says Fynn.

"Shouldn't we ration food?" This from Scarlett, at which we all scoff.

Fynn dives into his backpack and pulls out a Tupperware. "Annie," he says, waving the container at me. "Brought the cookies we made."

Oh yay. My mouth waters just thinking about the chocolate and peanut butter combination. He opens the container, grabs a couple, then sets it down and we all dive in. This is one of the things I love about Fynn: his baking.

Rocky and Beans aren't into it at all, but I love helping Fynn in the kitchen. Two weeks ago we made our very first coconut cake. Fynn's mom is always joking that one day we're going to open a bakery, and who knows, maybe Fynn will. But I'm not sure I like baking enough to do it for a job.

As he swallows one of Fynn's cookies, Beans goes

into his own backpack and pulls out snack bags of wheat crackers, almonds, and dried apples. He's the only kid I know who actually likes eating the healthy stuff his mom packs.

"You could've thought of us," Rocky jokingly gripes.

With a grin, Beans shoves a few crackers into his mouth. "Fine. More for me."

Fynn cringes at Beans's food. "The least you could do is use your big allowance to buy stuff we'll like, too."

Beans's smile fades, and I shoot Fynn a look. He picks the worst times to be all snarky.

Beans nudges his food away, unrolls his sleeping bag and slides inside. He turns his back on us and gets real still. I know he's not sleeping.

Fynn tosses a twig at Beans's head. "Hey." But when Beans grabs the stick off his head and chucks it away, Fynn just shrugs and says, "Drama."

Fynn has no clue what's going on with Beans, but I still defend him. "You know, you're one to talk, Fynn. At least the rest of us don't need to bring eighty billion different medicines on every trip. Talk about drama."

Fynn doesn't have a comeback. He just stares at

me while I stare back, and the more we stare, the more challenging and awkward the whole thing becomes. I was trying to defend Beans, and now I've managed to hurt Fynn's feelings. I should probably tell him I'm sorry.

"Um." Rocky looks between us. "Okay, change of topic. How about a drink? Anyone have anything?"

Slowly, Fynn drags his eyes off me, and as he digs around in his pack, I glance back over at Beans. I hope he tells them what's going on, because I don't want to repeat what just happened.

Fynn pulls a Capri Sun out and tosses it to Rocky, and he drinks it down in one long draw.

"Dipstick." Fynn throws his hands up. "Greedy much?"

Rocky sucks even harder on the straw, making that end-of-the-line gurgling sound. Fynn grabs another juice from his pack and makes a big show of drinking the whole thing, too. Rocky makes a grab for the pouch and Fynn dodges, and they both wrestle around for a few seconds.

Despite just being irritated with Fynn, I can't help but smile at the two of them as I glance over to Scarlett to see her smiling, too. Eventually, they stop with the juice war and Fynn tosses his empty Capri Sun at me. I toss it back and we make faces at each other, and that's our way of apologizing.

"So what's everyone doing this summer?" Scarlett asks.

"Football camp," Rocky answers.

"Vacation Bible School," Fynn says.

Beans doesn't answer, so I nod his way and answer for him. "Science camp."

"When Mom gets back from her honeymoon," Scarlett tells us, "we're moving into a new house. Then I'm going with a bunch of my friends to camp." She looks at me. "What about you?"

"My parents usually plan some sort of summer trip." I shrug. "Not sure. Dad mentioned Niagara Falls."

"Nothing with your friends?" Scarlett asks.

I wave my hand around. "You're looking at them," I say, and for the first time ever, I realize that they all have other friends and I don't.

It didn't used to be that way. We were one another's only friends. But over the past year, that's been changing. Rocky's got his football pals. Beans has his science friends. And Fynn's been getting more involved in his church youth group. I don't know, I could probably find some group to do something with, but I don't want to. I like what I've got here.

Rocky goes about unzipping his sleeping bag, and the rest of us follow, slipping inside ours. Snuggling down, I listen as Beans (always the first to fall asleep) begins breathing deeply. I hope he feels better in the morning.

My thoughts begin to rewind, and I get a little bummed thinking about my friends, and the other friends that they have and I don't. What will things be like a year from now? Will they still want to do Scouts things like this with me?

I roll my eyes. Of course they will. I'm being ridiculous.

With a sigh, I make myself not think about that and instead tune into my surroundings as night settles in, and I listen to the river and the crickets and a lone owl hooting. I wonder if we're still on Basinger's property. If not, then whose is it? And where, exactly, does the Mason Mountain Clan live? Not that I really believe they exist, but if I did—I glance around—where would they be?

Fynn swats his skin and I hear him squirting his bug repellent again.

"How did you guys become friends?" Scarlett whispers from beside me.

I think about kindergarten and how I met them pretty much the first day. We were learning to tie laces on our own shoes and then practicing on one another's. I caught the three of them tying a couple of kids' shoes together, and I jumped right in. We've been inseparable ever since.

But I don't tell Scarlett that story or any of the other crazy stuff we've done because they're my friends and I don't want to share them with anyone else. I don't say anything at all, hoping that she'll think I'm asleep.

"It's so cool you all are friends," she quietly says. "I don't have anything like this. I mean, I have friends, but none of them would ever do something like this with me."

Her words replay a few times in my head, and with each time I feel worse and worse. I've been kind of mean to her. Sounds like she might be lonely. Like her friends may be the fake kind. The kind where you're nice to one another's faces but mean behind your backs.

"Yeah," she whispers. "This is really great."

Gradually, everyone falls asleep, and as usual, I lie awake. I'm a night owl, as Dad says. My internal clock just won't turn off. Which makes getting up for school really crappy. Why can't school start at, say, noon?

Rolling over, I close my eyes and my thoughts zip and zing everywhere. The last day of school. Upcoming seventh grade. The summer ahead. This adventure. The river. I sigh. Why couldn't we have hiked up to a nice, calm, shallow place to cross?

Maybe I should get my flashlight and stroll down the bank a bit. See if there's a better place to cross. I slide out of my sleeping bag to do just that and catch sight of Rocky sitting over near the river's edge.

He looks so sad. So lonely. So different than earlier, wrestling with Fynn.

Quietly, I approach and sit down beside him. "Hey."

He gives me a little smile and goes back to looking at the river.

I don't say anything and just hang beside him as he stares into the dark water as it swirls around and over the boulders. The river really is pretty. Especially in the moonlight.

"Remember all those rafting trips we took when my mom was still alive?" he asks.

I smile. His mom was the greatest. This tiny Vietnamese woman with a big snorty laugh. With Rocky's hulking, huge dad, the two of them always looked so funny.

"Yeah," I answer. "I miss your mom."

He sighs. "I do, too."

Rocky never talks about his mom and so I'm not quite sure what to say. I know he misses her. Of course he misses her. And I know this has got to be the number one reason why he's not happy about his dad dating Fynn's mom. If they get married, Rocky will have a new mom and he doesn't want that. I get it.

"We used to tie, like, a dozen life jackets on you," Rocky says jokingly. "And you still wouldn't get out of the raft."

"It wasn't a dozen!" I laugh with him. It was probably close to a dozen.

A few seconds go by as our laughter slowly dies and we both go back to looking at the water. "I can't believe my dad is dating someone," he murmurs with such sadness in his tone that my heart twinges.

"At least Fynn's mom is nice," I say.

"Yeah. So nice she's been married twice before."

I hadn't thought about that. But is that what's

really bothering him, then? I don't know, but I try a different tactic. "If they get married, you would be stepbrothers. Fynn's one of your best friends."

Rocky doesn't answer and instead lies down in the grass and curls up on his side. "Think I might stay here for a little bit."

I think about his mother's funeral and what my mom said....

Holding my hand, Mom led me across the cemetery. We stopped walking a few feet from the Scouts, and she gave my hand a gentle squeeze. "Just be there for him," she quietly told me.

With a shaky breath, I stepped up beside them all, and Fynn looked over at me first. Then Beans, and we three exchanged a silent look.

Rocky just stared down at his mom's fresh grave.

Kneeling, I placed the daisies I'd picked next to the other flowers already there. Daisies were his mom's favorite.

Then I got back up, and the four of us stood quietly side by side, waiting for Rocky to decide when we would leave. It was the first time I can remember being together and never saying a word.

Just be there for him. That's what Mom said. So that's what I do as I lie down facing Rocky. "I'll hang with you," I tell him.

He smiles a little. "Thanks, Annie." And then he reaches out and does something he's never done before. He takes and holds my hand.

CHAPTER 5

Rocky closes his eyes and slowly drifts into sleep, and I lie here and stare at our joined hands. Something funny squirms around in my stomach, and I think about what Mom says about Dad. That she still gets butterflies with him. I've never really understood that whole butterfly thing, until now. It's supposed to be with someone you like, but this is Rocky. I don't like Rocky like that.

Do I?

I think about the way he's been acting around Scarlett, and, yeah, it irritates me, but that's not because I like Rocky and I'm jealous or something. It's because I don't like Scarlett. She's the one who annoys me. And frankly, I don't get why Rocky is all gooey over her. What's so great about her?

Is it just because she's pretty?

Rocky's hand slides from mine as he turns over, and I don't know how long I continue to lie here and look at his back, but eventually my mind slows down, and I yawn and let my eyes drift shut....

The sound of a crinkling wrapper wakes me up.

Slowly, I open my eyes and blink at the hazy morning sun trying to peek out from behind some clouds. I yawn and run my tongue around my mouth. Yuck. I hate morning mouth.

I sit up and reach for my pack and my toothbrush before I realize I'm still lying on the river's bank. I never went back to my sleeping bag last night. I look over to where Rocky's supposed to be to find an empty patch of grass. He must've left for his sleeping bag during the night. Dummy. Should've woken me up to do the same.

I hear more crinkling, and I turn my head. And I freeze.

A bear.

A bear. Yards away. On the other side of our camping spot. Clawing through our food. *A bear!*

I start to scoot away, and I keep right on scooting until I bump into someone. I don't look to see who it is as I move up and over the person until I'm on the other side.

"Ouch, Annie," Fynn grumbles. "What are you doing?"

I slam my hand over his mouth, and he looks straight up into my eyes.

Bear, I mouth very clearly, and watch his green eyes go wide. Slowly—very carefully—he slides from his sleeping bag, and I keep my gaze glued to the bear and the moon pie it's trying to get into.

I flick my attention over to Rocky's wadded-up sleeping bag to find it empty. Oh, my God. Did the bear drag him off? Images of big bear claws and gigantic teeth flash through my brain, along with visions of Rocky's mauled body, and I nearly hyperventilate.

Scarlett's gone, too. All of her stuff is gone!

Stealthily, Fynn crawls over to Beans, puts his hand over his mouth, and does the same thing I did—mouths, *Bear.* Beans isn't nearly as covert as he quickly scrambles out and up. The movement and the rustling catch the bear's attention and it glances up from the wrapper. I feel my eyelids freeze in place as I stare into the animal's black, round, ominous eyes.

In my peripheral vision I see Rocky step from the trees, and I nearly cry for joy. He's alive! "Holy hell," he whispers, and starts backing up into the trees he just came from.

The bear looks away from us and goes right back to the snacks, and I thank God those wrappers are childproof as the animal claws and tries to get at what's underneath.

"Annie," Fynn whispers from behind me. "Get over here."

I try to move, but I can't. It's like my body and my brain have completely frozen. Don't they say that when you see a bear, you should pretend to be dead? If that's true, I'm doing a great job.

The bear glances up from the food again and gives me a very long stare, and as I look into its eyes, I swear I can read its mind: *Mmm, that one looks tasty.* I stay frozen, mentally responding to the bear: *I promise those moon pies are way yummier than me.*

"Annie!" Beans whispers. "What are you doing?"

I feel something on my arm and jump before I

realize it's Fynn, and he's now pulling me back. "Come. On."

Slowly, very carefully, I get to my feet and start moving toward the woods. As I do, my gaze darts around our camping spot. Where's Scarlett?

"Up," Rocky quietly says, and I realize he's climbing a tree.

Beans starts scrambling up Rocky's tree, and Fynn and I scale the one beside it. Seconds later we're hidden in the limbs and leaves, staring down at the bear that I'm just now realizing isn't full grown. It's not a cub, though. More of a toddler, I guess. Not that it matters. It's still a bear! And Mama Bear can't be far.

I watch as the bear successfully finishes one snack and moves on to another.

"Where's Scarlett?" I whisper.

Fynn's eyes immediately flick down to her empty spot. "I don't know."

I look at Beans and Rocky, and they both helplessly shrug.

We go back to looking at the bear, but all I can think about is Scarlett. What if this bear, or maybe another one, dragged her off? But then, where's all of her stuff? It's not like a bear would neatly pack it up or something.

"It's leaving," Fynn says, and we all let out a collective relieved breath. The bear sidles off down the river, and as it rounds the corner and disappears, sunlight glints off something silver dusting its fur. I turn to ask the guys if they see it, too, when Fynn yells, "Scarlett!"

Silence.

"Scarlett!" Beans hollers.

Silence.

"Scarlett!" Rocky bellows.

Silence.

"SCARLETT!" I scream.

"What. Do. You. Want?" she snaps from the other side of the river.

I take in her dirty tank top, torn spandex, and tangled blond hair, and I nearly fall out of the tree with relief. "How did you get over there?"

She points up the river. "Downed tree. I crawled across. Why are you all in the trees?"

"Bear," Fynn calls over to her.

She jumps back. "What?"

"It's on our side," Rocky says. "Do you see it?"

Wildly, her head whips around. "No." She waves us over with both hands. "Get over here!"

"Are you sure you don't see it?" I ask.

"No! But hurry in case it comes back."

Good point. We scramble down, our gazes watching the area where the bear disappeared, and quickly gather our things. At least once we're over there with Scarlett, the river will be between us and the bear. Okay, maybe crossing the river isn't such a bad idea after all.

We follow Scarlett's directions, racing along beside the river, and sure enough, there's a tree that's fallen across. It looks fairly new, which is good. Not rotted.

But it's only about a foot in diameter. I crouch and look first at one end, then trail my eyes the twenty feet or so to the other. Both sides seem solidly wedged into the dirt banks.

I eye the water next, bubbling and swirling four feet or so below the tree, and uneasiness crawls through my guts.

Rocky turns and looks at me. "You can do this."

On the other side, Scarlett stands watching us. My uneasiness morphs into full-on nerves, and I start biting my thumbnail. "What if I slip?"

Rocky slides his backpack off, unzips it, and pulls

out some rope. "I'll tie you to me, and we'll cross together."

Beans steps up. "I can do it."

"Uh…" Rocky looks at me, and I know what he's thinking. Beans is no bigger than me. If I'm going to be tied to someone, I want it to be Rocky.

I give Beans a playful nudge. "Thanks, but Rocky's got it."

Beans gets all quiet and bummed and I feel horrible, but seriously, there's no way Beans could support my weight. Surely he knows that.

I watch as Rocky unravels the rope, and I get more and more nervous. My hands start to shake and I clench them to try to feel tougher. When he's done, he ties us together through our belt loops and gives both ends of the rope a good tug.

"We'll go first," he says. "Fynn and Beans, you follow."

Good idea. That way they can catch me if I slip.

"Who made you the boss?" Fynn grumbles, tucking in his shirt, and idly I wonder why he's tucking in his shirt. We're crossing a log. Does he think an untucked shirt is somehow going to make him ineligible for the neat and tidy award?

"Just do what he says," I say. "It's a good plan."

Then, in tandem, Rocky and I inch our way over the embankment and down onto the tree. It gives a little under our weight, and my whole body locks up.

Rocky crawls forward, but I don't follow. He glances back and lifts his dark brows, and I swallow an enormous anxiety-filled lump in my throat. "I felt it move," I tell him.

Fynn nudges me from behind. "It's okay. It's just settling in."

"It did that with me, too," Scarlett says from the other side of the bank.

I grit my teeth. "I don't need you being helpful right now." She's throwing it in my face that she crossed all by herself.

She holds her hands up. "Whatever."

Whatever.

I take a deep breath and blow it out and give Rocky a go-ahead nod. He starts to move forward again, and slowly, I make myself follow. Inch by inch we carefully crawl.

It did that with me, too.

And she's just one single person. But with the combined weight of all the Scouts...

The tree shifts a little on our bank, and my muscles cinch tight. "M-maybe Fynn and Beans should wait until we cross and then they can go."

"We're fine," Rocky assures me as he keeps crawling and the rope between us tightens. "Annie," he whines. "We need to keep moving."

The tree wobbles again, and all the air leaves my lungs. I halt, petrified.

"Annie!" Beans shouts from behind. "Move!"

But I can't. I'm frozen.

Another lurch, and this time the tree breaks free from the bank, and my world spins.

Our end drops four feet straight down into the water, and the other end precariously dangles from the bank as it clings to its roots.

Water rushes over me. Under me. Around me. It floods my mouth.

I cling to the tree and scream.

And choke.

And scream again.

We're going to die!

Then my body moves, and I realize Rocky is dragging me up the tree. Behind me, Fynn grunts as he wedges his shoulder into my butt and pushes. I hear Beans splash and gurgle, and I look over my shoulder to see him fighting his way up the tree behind Fynn and out of the water.

Someone death-grips my wrists and I swerve my gaze to see Scarlett dragging me the last few feet across the trunk. I'm dimly aware of the bark scratching my cheek. Then I'm on dry ground, still tethered to Rocky, and I dig my fingers into the dirt and gulp for air.

Beans starts throwing up—dry heaving, really. He does that when he's really scared. Wheezing cuts through the air next, and I jump into action, tugging Rocky along with me. I rip off Fynn's wet backpack, grab his inhaler, and push it into his hand.

Rocky begins untying us. "Annie, we have *got* to teach you to swim."

"Jesus." Fynn gasps for air. "We could have all died."

Tears well in my eyes and I angrily shove them away. "I'm sorry!"

Rocky dumps everything out of his backpack, and it's all soaked. As I'm sure all of our stuff is, too. He picks up his sopping wet sleeping bag and shoots me a look.

I jump to my feet. "Oh, y'all aren't so perfect!"

No one says anything for a few furious seconds as I loom in front of them, breathing heavily, my hands fisted and shaking. I yank the wet bandana off my head and throw it down.

Beans stops dry heaving, and Fynn stops wheezing as he unzips his pack and dumps out his stuff, too. I watch as he picks up a river-logged box of Band-Aids and tosses them aside. This is followed by all of his medicines. He opens a bottle of allergy pills, tilts it, and water pours out. I cringe. Maybe he should have sealed it better.

Fynn lifts fuming eyes to me. "If I get impetigo, you are so to blame."

"I'm sorry." I do feel bad.

Fynn keeps digging through his bag and pulls out—uh-oh—his Walkman. I watch as he holds it up and water dribbles from its seam.

Beans takes his portable player out of a waterproof case and holds it up. "No worries. I've got mine."

"'I've got mine,'" Fynn mimics. "Figures your Walkman is fine. This was my birthday present." He tosses the now useless thing onto the ground.

Scarlett intercedes, and for once I'm happy to hear her speak. "Let's lay everything out in the sun. I have something to show you all. And when we come back, it'll all be dry. Okay?"

"My Walkman will not be okay," Fynn snaps.

No one says anything to that, and I get a few more dirty looks.

"Yeah, okay," Rocky finally relents, and we lay our stuff out in the sun.

Still, no one speaks to me as we fall in step behind Scarlett. I really hate being the one they're mad at. I'm the one who referees *their* arguments. I'm not the one they're usually irritated with.

"What do you want to show us?" asks Beans.

Scarlett turns, and her green eyes dance with delight. "Just wait!"

CHAPTER 6

Scarlett pushes aside kudzu vines covering a hill. "Look what I found!"

Rocky folds his arms as he stares at the dark opening in the side of the hill. "Did you already go in?"

"Well, no." Scarlett grimaces. "I was too scared. I was waiting on you."

Rocky's mouth cocks up into a little macho smile.

She blushes. "All of you guys, of course."

Oh, my God. If I have to spend this whole trek watching the two of them flirting, I'm going to strangle myself. And then I'm going to strangle them. Wait. Make that the other way around. Them first, then me.

Plus, it was my hand he was holding last night. Not hers.

"What if there's someone in there?" Beans asks.

Crouching, I study the opening. It's big enough for an adult to crawl through. There could be someone in there. Or a wild animal. A bear. Yeah, there might be another bear.

"Hey, maybe it's like Indiana Jones," Fynn suggests. "And it's a trick cave with a treasure."

"Ooh," we all say.

And that's all it takes to have us simultaneously move toward the opening.

With our one and only waterproof flashlight, Rocky drops to all fours and takes the lead, like he usually does. I'm next, and Scarlett is right behind me.

"Smells like cat piss in here," Rocky says.

I inhale and immediately crinkle my nose. He's right.

The flashlight beam bounces off the dark walls and floor, and I get glimpses of dirt and twigs. The farther we crawl, the more the temperature drops and the dirt and twigs transition into mud. I went to Carlsbad Caverns a couple of years ago on our family vacation, but it was nothing like this. This cave looks like it's still undiscovered.

"This is a live cave," says Beans from behind.

"What's that mean?" asks Scarlett.

I want to remind her she won a science award and should probably know, but I don't.

"There's a water source," Beans answers. "Otherwise there wouldn't be mud."

"All I know is that it's nasty," mutters Fynn.

"What, are you afraid of getting your polo dirty?" I tease.

"Ha…ha…ha." Fynn's voice echoes around me, and I smile.

Rocky stops crawling, and I nearly run smack into his butt. He shines his light back and forth, illuminating whatever waits ahead. "That is so totally wicked," he says.

I peek around him and suck in a shocked breath. "Go." I give him a nudge. "I want to see."

He drops out of the passageway and into an enormous room that's about the size of half a football field.

Slowly, Rocky scans his light around the room and I take it all in—the walls glistening with dribbles of water; pointy rocks hanging from the ceiling; other ones growing up from the floor; and a small pool of water dead center in the room.

"Wow," Beans breathes once the whole gang has exited the passageway. "I bet this is just one room of a whole chain."

He snatches the flashlight out of Rocky's hand and walks the perimeter of the area as we fall in step behind him. "Stalactites and stalagmites." Beans points up and down. "Created by water and limestone drippings."

He swings the flashlight beam into our faces. "Don't touch them!"

I hold up my hands.

"Hey, hey, hey." Rocky jumps, kicking his Nikes. "R-r-rat!"

I hop back and look down to see an itty-bitty mouse scurry by. Rat? What rat?

"Where there's one," Fynn teases, "there will be others."

Rocky flips him the middle finger. He hates mice. One time he was at my house and we were in the kitchen. A baby mouse raced by, hovering along the baseboard, and Rocky nearly had a heart attack. He even jumped up on one of our kitchen chairs and squealed—actually squealed—like he was a little old grandmother or something.

I have no clue why he hates mice so much. I should ask him sometime. Then again, spiders freak me out, and I don't know why. They just do.

"Hello-o-o!" Beans calls, and his voice bounces all around us.

"Indiana Jo-o-ones!" I follow.

"Rocky loves mi-i-ice!" Fynn yells.

"Fynn's stu-u-upid!" Rocky shouts.

"La la-a-a," Scarlett finishes, and we laugh and listen as our voices ping-pong all around us before gradually becoming quiet again.

Then Beans stops walking. Rocky bumps into him. I bump into Rocky. And Scarlett and Fynn bump into me.

"Um..." Beans mutters, slowly backing up.

The flashlight beam shakes, and I follow its yellow glow all the way over to the wall, where something is on the ground. Something that looks an awful lot like a—

"Sk-sk-*skeleton*!" Fynn stammers.

Curiosity has my feet moving forward before they register I should probably be freaked there is a dead person right here. Rocky moves closer, too.

Holy moly. It *is* a skeleton.

With clothes. Overalls, to be exact, and a John Deere hat.

Reaching forward, I take the bill of its cap—

"What are you doing?" Scarlett gasps.

—and I lift off the hat. Beetles roll down its skull.

"Aaah!" I jump back, and the beetles disappear through the skeleton's eye sockets and gaped mouth.

Then something under its overalls moves. Something bigger than a beetle, and I watch in weird anticipation as whatever's under there slowly moves down the skeleton's denim-covered leg and emerges from the cuff.

Rocky leaps back as, yes, this time a small rat turns away from us and lumbers off into the dark. Clearly, it's not scared of us.

"Um, when was the last time any of you actually saw Old Man Basinger?" Beans asks.

I turn to him. "Why?"

He points his flashlight to the John Deere hat that I'm still holding. BILL BASINGER is printed in bold black marker on the inside.

I gasp. "Oh, no! This is Old Man Basinger. But how—" I glance back to his skeleton and a pang of sorrow hits me. I'm not sure why. It's not like I even knew him, and every time I did see him, he was mean.

But there was that time I saw him on his tractor parked under a tree reading an old paperback book.

And that time I saw him on a bench downtown smoking a pipe. Both times he'd seemed so normal and old. Like a grandfather.

But what about all the other times? Like when he chased us off his land because we were climbing his hay bales. And that time he yelled at us for building a snow dinosaur in his back pasture. And when he caught Rocky sneaking into his orchard and taking peaches for all of us.

Yeah, I guess we were annoying to the old guy. But he has the best land around here to play on. And it's not like we were destroying anything. We were just goofing around.

I hear something click and then wind, and I turn to see Beans taking pictures with a camera he had in a waterproof plastic bag. I don't know if he should be doing that. Isn't it wrong to take pictures of a skeleton?

"When we get back, we need to tell somebody we found him," Rocky says.

True. "But then that'll give away the fact we're out doing something we're not supposed to be doing."

"I can't get in trouble over this," Fynn says. "We'll do an anonymous letter or something."

We all nod and go back to pondering Old Man

Basinger. A few seconds later I put his hat back onto his skull and adjust the brim so it's sitting a little cocked, like I imagine he would wear it.

Beans crouches down and studies him for a couple of long seconds. "The bones seem awfully clean. Where's the skin and the decay?"

I cringe. "Yuck."

"Maybe the beetles picked it clean," Rocky says, and Beans gives a thoughtful nod.

"Okay, gross." Scarlett gags. "Stop talking about it."

"What do you suppose he was doing in here?" Fynn asks. "Wait a minute. Do you think someone put him in here? Do you think someone *murdered* him?"

No one says anything for a good solid moment as the enormity of that question sinks in. *Murder?* Uneasiness creeps up my backbone and I swallow a lump of dread in my throat. Does his family know he's missing? Surely they have to know by now. Judging from his skeleton, he's been here awhile.

I think about Beans's question and try to remember the last time I saw Old Man Basinger. I think it's been about a month. He's been missing a month? Why haven't any of us heard about it?

"Or maybe it was just old age," Rocky quietly says. "The guy was ancient."

Old age. Murder.

I like *old age* a lot better.

"It could have been the Mason Mountain Clan." Fynn grabs the flashlight and shines it in Beans's face. "I told you they're real. They killed him and stowed his body in here."

I suck in a breath. He's right. They could've killed Old Man Basinger.

Beans holds his hand up against the light and with a tolerant look says, "Don't be ridiculous. There is no Mason Mountain Clan."

"But you don't know for sure," I say.

Suddenly a loud fluttering fills the air. Like flapping wings in stereo, times a million.

Scarlett backs away. "Wha-a-at is that?"

The noise gets louder. Louder. And louder. Then out of I-don't-know-where come a zillion bats. Flipping and flapping and spiraling through the air like a black tornado.

Fynn drops the flashlight and it rolls across the cave floor. The beam bounces off the bats' bodies, and distorted shadows swirl across the walls of the cave.

One of them dive-bombs me, and I shout, "Run!"

I manage to snatch the flashlight off the floor, and

we take off sprinting across the cave, slipping and sliding and screaming and pushing against one another. Fynn dives into the passageway first. Then Scarlett and me, followed by Rocky and Beans. I move faster than I think I probably ever have in my life.

"Go!" Beans shouts, shoving all of us from behind.

The beating wings echo around us in the crawl space as we frantically fight our way toward the daylight, finally scrambling from the hole.

"Ohmygod, ohmygod, ohmygod," Scarlett chants hysterically, dancing around as Fynn shakes his arms like he's got the heebie-jeebies.

Gripping the flashlight, I lean my hands on my knees and try to catch my breath. I've never seen a bat that close up before!

"Those were real," Beans says to us all, like we didn't just see the flying bloodsuckers.

More calm than he should be, Rocky folds his arms and surveys us. "What a bunch of wimps."

"What?" I yell. "You were running, too!"

Rocky huffs. "Not even."

Scarlett holds her hands up. "You remember I was talking about a rabid squirrel earlier? There was also this bat—"

Beans interrupts her. "Bats really won't hurt you. They work off sound. We were too loud. We disturbed them." His eyes get really big and excited. "Let's go back in and look around some more."

Scarlett shakes her head. "I'm not going back in there."

Fynn backs up. "Me neither. Clearly, you don't know what kind of diseases they carry."

I pause, watching Fynn and Scarlett disappear into the trees, thinking now that I'm out here (and calmer) and I know what's in there—a really cool cave, Basinger's skeleton, and bats that will calm down soon—yeah, okay, I'll go back.

"Let's do this," Rocky says. "Just the three of us."

I nod. "I'm in."

But then Scarlett's scream cuts through the trees, and we take off running.

CHAPTER 7

"All our stuff is gone!" Scarlett screeches, and all I can do is stand in complete dumbfounded shock, staring at the patch of sunny grass where we left everything.

Everything.

My purple pocketknife. Our waterlogged flashlights. Sleeping bags. What little food we had left. My favorite bandana. Beans's map.

Oh, no, the map!

Fynn and Beans stomp up and down the bank of the river, yelling and throwing their hands up. Rocky charges into the woods looking for, I assume, whoever took our stuff. Scarlett keeps screeching. And I can't seem to move. My dad gave me that pocket-knife just yesterday.

"You kids okay?"

I whip around to see a boy standing across the river. Shirtless with jeans and boots, he wears a ball cap backward and has dark hair. I'd say he's probably sixteen.

And he's really cute.

Really cute. Wait a minute, where did that thought come from?

Fynn, Beans, and Scarlett stop what they're doing and turn to look at him. The boy smiles, and I feel my face get hot.

"You kids okay?" he repeats.

"Someone took all of our stuff!" Scarlett screeches. I really wish she would stop with the screeching.

Rocky comes barreling back out of the woods and halts to a stop. The boy across the river takes us all in, and I can only imagine what we must look like. Fynn's penny loafers, Scarlett's torn spandex, my matted hair, Rocky's bloody knee, and Beans's muddy high-waters. Yeah, I'm sure we look like we know what we're doing.

"What kind of stuff?" he asks.

"Your dog only has three legs," Beans says instead,

and I just now realize there's a small white and black mutt standing beside the boy. With, sure enough, only three legs.

The dog cocks his head and wags his tail. Aw. Super cute. Just like his owner.

The boy leans down and pats the dog's head. "This is Hoppy. My name's Edge."

"Edge," Rocky mumbles. "What kind of name is Edge?"

"What kind of name is Rocky?" I mumble back, and earn a glower.

"Where you kids headed?" Edge asks.

"To the me—"

Beans slaps his hand over Fynn's mouth. "Nowhere. Just out playing."

Edge gives us another perusal, and his lips twitch like he thinks we're funny.

"I heard screaming a few minutes ago. Are you sure everything's okay? You haven't seen anything odd, have you?"

"Just act casual," Rocky mutters before shouting, "Nope! We're fine."

"All right. Well, you kids be safe. There are a lot of dangers in the woods." With that, Edge and Hoppy sidle off.

Fynn shoves Beans. "Don't ever put your nasty hand on my mouth."

"You were going to blow our cover," Beans says.

I keep watching Edge all the way until he disappears around the bend of the river. He was definitely cute. Scarlett sighs, and I turn to see her watching him, too. I narrow my eyes. Hey, now.

Rocky scoffs. "I bet he took our stuff."

"How is that even possible?" I defend a cute boy I don't even know. "He's over there. We're over here. There's a whole river between us. And 'act casual'? What was that all about?"

"I swear, have I not taught you all anything over the years? People are suspicious when you don't act normal, casual, like you're supposed to be doing whatever it is you're doing. Now, listen," Rocky says. "Whoever took our stuff couldn't have gotten far. We need to track them down and get everything back."

"But what if the people who took our stuff are mean?" I ask the obvious question.

No one responds to that, and then Fynn quietly says, "Like the Masons."

I swallow. He's right. And if not the Masons, then someone equally despicable.

Beans sighs. "How many times do I have to tell

you the Masons don't exist? Here's the thing"—he takes on this rational tone that he sometimes uses on us, like he thinks it will convince us to believe whatever he is telling us—"we were in the cave. Our stuff was out here. Whoever wandered by probably thought our stuff had been abandoned. We'll ask for it back and they'll give it because they ultimately didn't realize it belonged to someone. Okay?"

I glance over to Fynn and catch his skeptical look. Good, he's not buying this plan, either.

"I think we should go home," Scarlett says.

I agree. She should go home.

"I could take you," Rocky volunteers, and I groan.

"Besides," Rocky says. "This trip is too dangerous for a lady."

I snort. A *lady*? "Now, wait a minute. You can't leave. The Scouts are supposed to be in this together."

"But I'm not a Scout," Scarlett says.

Correct, which means she should go home. I want to point across the river and to the way home, but if I do, I'm pretty sure Rocky will leave with her, and that will just stink. It's all or none. It's always been all or none.

Okay. Whether I like it or not, Scarlett is coming.

So I change tactics. "Look, the tree fell, so you can't get back across the river. Let's just—"

"We're stranded!" Scarlett slams her hands over her heart. "We don't have any food, or water, or the map. We're going to die out here!" Her bottom lip wobbles.

Rocky puts his arm around her, and something prickly and jealous curls through me. "Don't cry," he says. "We'll just walk upriver and find a new spot to cross. Then we'll go home."

Scarlett sniffles, and I swear I see her bat her lashes. "Are you sure?"

"Fine!" I shout, throwing my hands up. "Be a bunch of babies. All of y'all go home. I'll find the meteor without you." I stomp off, hoping to God I'm going in the right direction.

This just stinks. This adventure was supposed to be great, and so far nothing is great about it. Between Scarlett coming along, the bear that nearly ate us, me almost drowning, losing all of our stuff, finding dead Old Man Basinger, being attacked by bats, Rocky being all sullen about his dad dating Fynn's mom, and Beans's bad news, this has been no fun at all.

Speaking of, Beans should be the one insisting we

keep going. He should tell them we need to find the meteor, sell it for some money or get a reward or something, so he can stay here and not have to move in with his dad. He should be right here stomping with me. Because, frankly, I'm about ready to go home, too.

They can do their football camp and Vacation Bible School and science thing. I'll find some new friends. Ones that won't be a pain in my butt.

"Is she going the right way?" I hear Fynn ask Beans.

"Yeah," he says. "She is."

Good. At least there's that.

I keep right on stomping, putting all my temper into each step. Scarlett is definitely ruining everything. Rocky would never try to abandon us if she weren't here. And, again, why won't Beans just tell everyone what's going on with his mom and his house?

I don't know how much time goes by, but somewhere up the river I realize I'm not stomping anymore, and I also realize my friends are behind me.

"I hear in seventh grade we have to start taking showers after PE," Fynn says. "I don't know about you, but I'm not getting naked."

"What, are you afraid of everyone seeing your small wiener?" Rocky teases.

"Shut up!" Fynn says, and Scarlett giggles.

Beans falls in step beside me. "Thanks," he whispers.

I glance over at him. "Why don't you just tell them?"

"Because, Annie, I don't want to. Okay?"

I try to think about it from Beans's point of view—like if we were losing our house—but I would definitely tell Rocky and Fynn. I wouldn't keep it a secret from my friends.

Scarlett pipes up from right behind me. "Edge was so cute. I've got a major thing for older boys."

Inside, I smile. I hope Rocky's paying attention, because he's definitely not older.

Fynn sniffs. "He wasn't that cute."

I grin over my shoulder. "Jealous someone's prettier than you?"

"No." Fynn makes a face at me.

"Yes, you are."

"No, I'm not."

"No, you're not."

"Yes, I—" Fynn pauses. "Hey!"

I laugh, feeling more like myself now. "I get you every time with that."

"I'm hungry," Beans gripes, which makes my own stomach growl.

"Wish we still had some of my cookies," Fynn says.

Me, too. "Actually, I wish we had some of your brownies. The ones with macadamia nuts and chocolate chunks on top."

Everyone groans. Yep, Fynn does make some good brownies. Well, except for that time he made an Ex-lax batch...

Fynn got on the bus carrying a baggie of brownies and plopped down in our usual seat.

Beans and Rocky and I all lit up. "Ooh, can we have one?"

Fynn shook his head. "Nope."

I folded my arms. "You're mean."

Gary, the bus bully, reached over the seat and shoved Fynn in the head. "Boys aren't supposed to make brownies."

"Now, wait a minute!" I started to defend Fynn and he shot me a look. I knew that look. He was up to something.

Gary snatched the brownie bag from Fynn's hands.

"Hey," Fynn protested halfheartedly as Gary tore open the bag, grabbed a handful, and shoved them into his big mouth.

With a sneaky smile, Fynn settled down beside us.

Beans lifted his brows. "Well?"

"Ex-lax," Fynn whispered, and we all snickered.

Gary didn't stop his caveman ways, but he never stole food from any of us again.

Voices floating through the trees cut through my memory and bring us to a stop.

"Them there stupid kids." A man's phlegmy laugh echoes through the morning, and we stop to listen. "Leavin' all that stuff out fer us to git."

A woman's cackle follows the man's, and the deep, raspy sound of it makes me swallow hard. That cackle does not sound like it comes from a very nice woman. "Maybe we's need to teach 'em a good ol'-fashioned Mason lesson."

"Guys," Fynn whispers in terror. *"It's the Mason Mountain Clan!"*

CHAPTER 8

Rocky motions for us to drop to our hands and knees, and together we crawl forward to peek through the bushes and into a clearing. Why we crawl forward, I'm not sure. It makes much more sense to go in the other direction. But the Scouts and I aren't always so great about using common sense.

There's a campfire with a few tree stumps around it in the middle of the clearing. Over to the right sits a trailer with a porch hanging half on, half off. Beside that stands a big black tank with hoses in the top and a valve sticking out the front.

Nearby looms a huge junk pile with an old wagon wheel, a large cracked vase, a rusted bike, a car frame painted with blue and yellow daisies, a hanging wind chime made out of assorted chunks of pottery, a rocking chair with only two slats on the back, a mounted deer head with one eyeball, and so many other things, it's impossible to figure out what it all is.

Honestly, it's all kind of cool, and under other circumstances I might enjoy exploring the junk pile.

Rocky whispers, "I heard the Mason Clan cuts the heads off kids and sticks them on poles in their front yards."

Fynn murmurs, "And they make stew of the kids' meat and bones."

Beans swallows. "I'm going to throw up."

Scarlett's eyes go wide. "Let's get out of here!" she whispers.

I shoot Beans a dirty look. "We told you the Mason Clan existed."

"Who cares who said what?" Rocky mumbles.

"I'm going to throw up." Beans swallows again.

Obviously the Mason Mountain Clan is not something our parents made up. They are real, and they are right there, just yards away. We need to get out of here. I point back the direction we came and start crawling away.

Behind me, Fynn gasps for air.

Not now! I turn to look at him. "Don't have an asthma attack!" I whisper.

"Well, whatter we have 'ere?"

My friends scream, and I freeze.

Then slowly, very carefully, I turn my head, and I drag my gaze over two black rubber boots, up a couple of very big hairy legs, past a dirty flowered dress, around an impressive gut, and into the face of the most enormous woman I have ever seen. From behind her steps a man and three teenage boys.

"What're you just standin' there fer?" says the woman. "Grab 'em!"

I move quickly, trying to scramble away, but she bends over and snatches my arm. One of the boys gets Scarlett. Another, Beans. The man snags Fynn. And as the other boy lunges for Rocky, he takes off sprinting in the other direction.

"Rocky!" I shout, but he doesn't turn around as he races through the trees and disappears. What is he doing? He can't let them take us! "Rocky!" I yell again, hoping to God he's running for help.

The Mason Clan drags us in the other direction, flailing and screaming through the woods.

I claw at the woman's meaty hand, twisting and writhing my body. "Let me go!"

"Shut up," she snaps, giving me a hard shake.

I catch glimpses of trees, sky, my friends, the woman's dress, leaves, a pile of stuff, a shed, a lawn chair, a slow-burning fire, a bag of Twinkies. My guts whirl. What are they going to do to us?

And then she slings me forward, and I go sliding into a skunky-smelling, shadowy shed.

Fynn lands on top of me. Then Scarlett. Then Beans.

Cackling, the woman slings the metal door closed, and whatever daylight was in there goes out.

Scarlett screams.

Beans projectile vomits.

Fynn wheezes for air.

And I start crying.

CHAPTER 9

I have no clue how much time has gone by. All I know is that it's hot in here and I've bitten all my nails down so far that my pinky has started to bleed. I wish Fynn still had his Band-Aids.

Speaking of Fynn, he's currently huddled in the back of the shed with Scarlett, being absolutely no help. I'm sure he's probably imagining every germ in this place. Beans, though, he's next to me, peering through a crack in the wall, surveying the area. I hope his brilliant brain is spinning a way out of this.

The Masons are sitting around their campfire, and now that I'm not being dragged along the ground, I have a chance to get a better look at them. The woman is indeed enormous. She's taller than my dad, and he's six two. She's bigger than my Aunt Susie, who I heard Mom say is three hundred pounds. And her red hair sticks out all over the place, looking like it hasn't been brushed in the past year.

Two of the boys are short and pudgy, and the third one is tall and skinny. That one, the skinny one, sits off by himself over on the porch steps. The man is skinny, too, with a long ponytail and a mustache so bushy, I seriously would not be shocked if something crawled out of it. He's sitting on one of the stumps around the fire, whittling a stick with a pocketknife.

Hey, wait a minute. That's my pocketknife!

And then I see it. All of our stuff. Sitting in a pile behind the woman. From the looks of it, they've already picked through everything. How dare they! That's ours!

Then I notice the silver dusting the roof of their shack, and I suddenly remember the bear. I give Beans a nudge. "Check out the roof. That silver dust was on the bear, too. It's the same stuff that was in our hair when we climbed down from the silo. From the meteor, right?"

Beans frowns for a second while he thinks. "Yeah,

it must be. Like the meteor is leaving a bread crumb trail for us to follow."

I turn around and look at everything crammed in the shed with us. It's just more of what's outside. Junk. Where do they get all this stuff? Do they steal it? And what do they do with it? By the looks of the rust and dust, nothing.

Crawling across the dirt, I start picking through the pile, looking for…I'm not sure what. A weapon, maybe? My stomach pitches at the thought. I never imagined I'd want to use a weapon, but I'm not going to let these people hurt my friends.

"Help me look," I say to Fynn and Scarlett. There's got to be something in here that can help us escape.

I come across a book bag and my fingers pause. The Mason Mountain Clan are rumored to kidnap and eat kids. Maybe they throw the kids' stuff in here afterward? Who did this book bag belong to? I wonder, as I swallow a sudden lump and imagine what people might find of us one day: Fynn's inhaler, my pocketknife, Scarlett's lip gloss, Beans's compass, and Rocky's muscle tee.

I hope Rocky's out there looking for help.

With shaky hands I slide the book bag closer,

unzip it, and look inside. It's empty. I hold it up to a shaft of light filtering through the slats in the shed, looking for a name tag or something, and feel oddly relieved there's nothing identifying whom it once belonged to. Like if the book bag is anonymous, then maybe the Mason Clan just found it. They didn't actually kill a kid to get it.

Something over to the right catches my attention next, and I reach past several hubcaps and pull it free. The hubcaps clank together as I do, and I put my hands on them to keep them quiet. For a second I don't move, my ears tuned to the outside, but I hear only the crackle of the fire.

"What'd you find?" Scarlett whispers.

"I don't know." It's a long, dusty, brown leather case. I lay it down on the dirt floor, unsnap it, and flip it open to see a shotgun lying inside. My eyes snap up to Beans, and his go wide as he stares down at the gun.

"Is it loaded?" Fynn asks.

I shake my head. "I don't know. I don't know anything about guns."

Beans scoots over and leans in to study the silver engraved tag. He squints and rubs his finger over the dirty writing. " 'Basinger,' " he whispers, and I suck in a shocked breath. They really did kill him.

"They're responsible," Fynn says. "This is proof. Why else would they have his gun?"

I think of that time I saw Old Man Basinger on his farm, holding a shotgun propped on his shoulder and looking for us. My friends and I were giggling and hiding behind a wall of trees. We knew we weren't supposed to be there. We were playing our own ridiculous version of Basinger hide-and-seek.

Yeah, we can be real idiots.

Scarlett reaches for the shotgun. "I know about guns."

I look up to Fynn to see if she's telling the truth, and he nods. "Her mom takes her shooting."

Wow, a dad who's a band manager and a mom who shoots. That's gnarly.

Scarlett lifts the shotgun out of the case. "Let me see if there're any bullets."

Any bullets. Meaning we may use this to defend ourselves. We may have to shoot this thing. We might even have to shoot one of the Masons.

I think I'm going to be sick.

Scarlett presses something, slides something else, and cocks open the gun. I watch as she looks it over, and I am filled with both hope and dread and a little bit of awe that she actually knows what she's doing.

Then she clicks the gun back together and puts it in its case. "No bullets."

I feel more relief than anything as I close the case. I really didn't want to have to shoot someone. As I slide the gun back toward the pile of junk, voices filter in from outside, and I scoot back over to the crack in the shed and peer out.

"Ya think they's looking for that thing that fell from the sky?" asks one of the chubby brothers.

"It's called a meteor," answers the skinny one.

" 'It's called a meteor,' " the first one mimics, and then gives him a hard shove. "Shut up, Junior!"

The third brother laughs. "Maybe we should teach you just how smart you really ain't."

"Yuns all shut up," the woman snaps. "Fact is, them others are after it, too."

I look at Beans. *Others? What others?* I mouth, and he shrugs. We go back to looking through the crack.

The woman plants her hands on her hips and looks over at the shed, and I duck back. "Otis, I'm tellin' ya. Them kids know somethin' they's not supposed to."

We do?

She pulls our map from her front dress pocket and snaps it against her palm. "You seen them *X*s?" she says to the man, who I now know is named Otis. "Yep, I's got a feelin' some'in' else is going on. Why's so many people looking fer this thing?"

"Who else would be looking for it?" Beans whispers, and I shrug. The big woman's right. Something's going on.

"We's gonna leave 'em right here and go find this thing," she tells the man.

Otis strikes my pocketknife against that stick of wood and turns his beady eyes over to the shed. "Maybe they just after our moonshine," he says.

The woman snarls, and I swear I hear a growl. "Wouldn' be the first."

"We're not after your moonshine!" Beans yells.

I slap him on the shoulder. "Would you shut up?"

"We's gonna find out." The woman stomps over to the shed, and the four of us scramble into the back corner, next to all the junk. She fiddles with the lock and throws the door open, and fresh air rushes in.

Towering in the doorway, she glowers over at Beans's pile of throw-up. "Which one of you brats did that?"

I resist the urge to jab my finger in Beans's direction. Fynn does instead, and I shoot him a warning glare.

She plants her fists on her meaty hips. "Now, which one of yuns we gonna work on first?"

Fynn's entire body begins violently shaking.

Scarlett's nails dig into the skin of my arm.

Beans scoots farther back, up and over the junk.

The woman's eyes track across each one of us, before landing on Fynn.

"N-n-no. Please." He wheezes, and I know he's about to go into a full-on attack. "Please leave us alone."

She points at him. "You. Get out 'ere."

"Please," I beg her. "He has asthma. Leave him alone."

Her narrowed gaze slides from Fynn over to me. "Then you. Come on."

CHAPTER 10

My throat tightens, and I swallow. "Wh-wh-what are you going to do to me?"

She snarls, like she's some kind of rabid ferret. "If you don't git out 'ere right now, I'll string up every one of yuns kids."

I don't immediately move. I don't think I can.

"You hear me, girl?"

I make myself nod, and as I stiffly go to get up, Beans clings to me. "No, Annie."

"I-it's okay," I mutter, pushing the rest of the way to stand, and digging my fingertips into my palms, I shuffle my feet across the dirt floor toward the woman.

She snatches me as soon as I reach the doorway, slams shut and locks the metal shed, then drags me across the leaves and sticks of their yard. I stumble behind her, my blood hammering, desperate to scream, to fight, to do *something*, but trying so very hard to be brave.

Otis sucks his teeth. "Now, Mary Jo, don' go and do anythin' too stupid."

She cackles and gurgles up a loogie that she spits. I cringe. *Ick.*

Mary Jo shoves me down into the dirt. "Stay."

Wildly, I look around. I could run. I could totally run. Two of the Mason boys take a step toward me like they can read my mind, but I notice that the skinny one, the one they were picking on, hangs back. Junior, they called him.

But before I have time to react to anything, Mary Jo crams me inside a large canvas sack, leaving my head and arms sticking out the top. She cinches it tight under my armpits and ties my hands behind my back. Then two of her boys hoist up the sack with me in it, and the next thing I know, I'm hanging from a tree limb.

I squirm and kick at the sack. "Let me down!"

Mary Jo crows with laughter and Otis joins in. One of the boys pokes me with a stick.

"I say we ransom 'em," Otis says.

Mary Jo gives that considerable thought. "Kidnap 'n' ransom. We're some real outlaws, you 'n' me."

Kidnap and ransom? My heart bangs a terrified beat that goes straight into full-on racing.

"Ma," Junior says. "You know—"

"Kidnap 'n' ransom." Mary Jo steps up and gets right in my face. "Whaddaya think of that, li'l girl? You think yuns parents will pay money for ya?"

I think of yesterday when Mom and Dad were in my bedroom. I had thrown that dress on the floor. I'm horrible. Mom spent money on that dress and I tossed it on the floor. My eyes blur with tears. Ransom? My parents don't have money to pay a ransom for me.

One of the boys puffs out his bottom lip. "Look, Ma, you made her cry."

"What is wrong with you all?" I blurt out. "We're just a bunch of kids. We were out having fun and camping—" My voice cracks, and I can't stop the tears that fall. I take a few shaky breaths and look at the Masons as they silently stare back at me.

None of them mutter one single word, and while the quiet grows, my mind spirals. *What are they going to do to me now? Why are they just watching me?*

Mary Jo snaps out of her staring, and she pulls the map out of her dress pocket and shoves it in my face. "What're the *X*s?"

I don't respond. That meteor's supposed to save Beans. If these people find it instead, Beans is definitely leaving.

She shoves the map in my face again. "Speak, girl."

My bottom lip wobbles. I can't tell them. I can't.

Mary Jo sneers. "I'll go get your friends. I'm sure one of 'em'll talk. The wheezy one will."

Not Fynn! He'll have a full-on attack, and these people won't know to give him his inhaler. The words tumble from my lips. "It's just a meteor that fell. I promise. We thought we might find it. That's all. I'll tell you anything you want to know. Just don't hurt us."

She glares at me, like she's trying to figure out if I'm telling the truth, and then she points at the two short boys. "You two come with me. We're gonna find that one that got away."

"Run, Rocky!" I shriek so loudly my vocal cords spasm. *Please be near and hear me.* "Run!"

Mary Jo slaps her hand over my mouth, and I catch my breath and gag. Her hand stinks! She sticks her jowly face right in mine, and my eyeballs zero in on her beady blue ones. A moment thumps by and I absolutely regret screaming for Rocky. Her mouth curls into a dirty grin. I know I'm done for.

Without saying a word to me, she flops her hand out toward one of the boys. "Bandana."

Bandana? What is she going to do, blindfold me?

In my peripheral vision I see one of the brothers untie a purple bandana from his neck. Hey, that's mine! He hands it to her and she proceeds to cram it into my mouth. I gag and gasp and shake my head and poke at it with my tongue and gag some more. After being on the boy's sweaty skin, it tastes like rot, and I can't get it out of my mouth!

With a chuckle, Mary Jo and two of the boys amble off through the woods, and Otis settles down into a rusted lawn chair. He crosses his booted feet, slides his hat down over his face, and folds his arms over his skinny stomach.

"Go round me up some pork rinds," he tells Junior.

The boy looks at me for a second in this hesitant way, like he's trying to figure out what to do. I hold my breath, keeping my eyes locked on his, hoping he's about to let me go. But then he turns and hurries to the trailer, and I let out a frustrated breath.

A moment ticks by, and then Otis's snore begins vibrating through the air.

I look over to the shed to see Beans, Fynn, and Scarlett all peering out at me through the gap in the metal slats. I squirm and kick and strain at the ties around my wrists and get absolutely nowhere.

Dipping my head, I run my mouth and the bandana back and forth across the canvas sack, and the friction tugs the bandana loose. I spit it out and spit some more, trying to clean my mouth. Eck. Nasty.

Craning my neck, I look up at the tree limb. It's really not that thick. It should snap. I bounce my body. Once. Twice. Three times. And the limb merely bounces with me.

Looking back over at the shed, I catch sight of my friends' fingers sticking out of every gap they can find, trying the slats for looseness, and an idea forms.

"See if you can dig out underneath," I whisper, but I know they can't hear me over Otis's snores.

"See if you can dig out underneath," I say a little louder, but my friends still don't hear me.

"Hey!" I call out, and all three of them look through the slats at the same time Otis chokes on a snore.

I freeze, and my pulse ping-pongs around in the canvas sack.

One second goes by. Then another. And Otis bumps right back into sawing up the area.

I swerve my gaze over to my friends again. "Try. To. Dig. Out. Un-der-neath," I whisper, dramatically moving my lips so they can be read.

I wait, my gaze glued to the bottom of the shed. Then I see it: slight movement, a stirring of dirt. They're digging. They're digging!

I crane my neck as far left as I can toward the Masons' shack, silently praying Junior doesn't come back out. Then something a little beyond the shack catches my attention. A shadow. A movement in the trees.

Oh, no. Mary Jo's already coming back!

But it's Rocky who steps through the trees with his finger over his mouth, and I grin with pure joy and relief, and then grin even bigger when Edge and Hoppy follow right behind him.

The boys both eye Otis as they tiptoe past the Masons' shack toward me. When they're right in front, I whisper, "Beans and Fynn and Scarlett are in the shed."

Edge and Rocky turn to the shed to see my friends' fingers sticking out of the cracks in the metal slats. Luckily, they know enough not to make any sound. Or rather, Scarlett knows enough not to screech for help.

"Where's the key?" Edge whispers to me.

"I don't know. But hurry. One of the boys is inside the shack, and Mary Jo and the other two went off looking for Rocky."

Edge pulls a large hunting knife from a holder strapped to his hip. He wraps one arm around me and the canvas potato sack I'm contained within, and as he holds me and saws at the rope connecting me to the tree, I try very hard to ignore the fact he's *holding* me.

With a soft grunt and one last whack by Edge, my rope breaks free and Edge lowers me to the ground. He loosens the sack and rolls me over to cut the ties around my wrists.

Otis chokes on another snore, and the three of us jump into action. We sprint around him and the fire pit and start digging at the earth beneath the shed where my captive friends have already put a tiny dent. Hoppy gets into it, too, clawing at the ground. Beans, Fynn, and Scarlett feverishly work from their side, and little by little the ground begins to break free. But it's taking forever!

I shoot a hurried glance over my shoulder to make sure Mary Jo isn't by some horrible chance standing right behind me, and I see all the junk strewn across the yard. Racing over, I find a scrap of metal, a rusted spade, and a hunk of wood. I run back to Rocky and Edge, hand out the junk, and we all keep right on plowing.

Otis smacks his lips, and I glance over to see him shift positions before he goes right back on with sleeping.

Dirt kicks up as we claw and dig and scratch at the ground. I don't know how dogs do it. It's harder than it seems. It feels like we've been digging forever, but the hole still isn't through to the other side.

"Otis!" I hear Mary Jo bellow in the distance, and nerves punch through me.

"Hurry," I say.

A cough comes from behind, and I whirl around to see Junior standing behind us, holding the bag of pork rinds. I get ready to lunge and tackle him in defense, but then he holds his finger to his mouth. "Shh."

I freeze in place, carefully eyeing him as he walks over to a nearby tree, reaches behind it, and brings out a key. "Mom keeps an extra one here," he whispers.

A key! He's helping us?

Holding it up, he smiles as he walks it toward us, and I don't think twice now as I hurry over, snatch it from his fingers, and quickly unlock the shed.

My friends tumble out.

"Get our stuff!" I whisper, motioning to the pile, and while they do, I carefully look all around Otis, but I don't see my pocketknife anywhere.

Dad's going to kill me.

I hear Junior locking the shed, and I turn. "Thank you," I quietly say. "I can't believe you helped us."

With a shy smile, he looks down at the ground, and I feel sorry that he has to live here with these mean people. Maybe after all of this is over, I can try to be his friend. Though I'm not sure how that will work, but surely my friends and I can figure something out.

I hear leaves rustling and turn my head to see Mary Jo emerge from the trees.

She takes one look at the scene and charges straight toward us. "GIT BACK HERE!"

CHAPTER 11

We tear off into the trees, thrashing our way through the foliage, jumping downed limbs and tripping over rocks. The Masons are behind us, yelling, whacking their way through the woods. Oh, my God, do they have machetes? Surely Mary Jo can't run that fast with all her weight. It's got to be the boys.

I don't look back. I just run. Run. And keep running, with my eyes glued to Edge ahead of me. Blindly, I follow him. I have no clue how far we go, but it must be at least a mile. Somewhere in the back of my brain I think, *Man, I'm glad our PE teacher makes us sprint laps.*

Edge finally stops, and gasping for air, the rest of us do, too.

"Oh." Beans dry heaves. "My." Dry heave. "Lord."

Rocky leans over, bracing his hands on his knees. "Did—" He sucks in a lungful of air. "Did we go far enough?"

I fall down onto the ground, gasping for air. I'm going to hyperventilate. Just like Fynn. I have got to calm down. Or use his inhaler.

Breathe, I tell myself. It's okay. We're okay. We got away.

Beans falls down beside me, and while we both continue to get our breathing under control, I tune in to our surroundings. To the shade of the trees and the sound of the river somewhere to the right. To a bug or two buzzing about and the slight breeze. To the scent of damp earth. I don't hear anything but nature. Yep, I think we lost them.

Edge lowers himself down to sit against a tree with an exhausted Hoppy panting at his feet.

I lever up on my elbows, looking around, realizing… "Where're Scarlett and Fynn?"

Rocky straightens up. "I thought they were right behind me."

Oh, no. "Scarlett!" I scream, rolling to my knees.

Beans sits up, too. "Fynn!"

"Shut up," Rocky whispers. "The Masons could hear you."

I press my lips together. He's got a point. We have no clue where the Masons are. If we completely lost them. If they turned back. Luckily, they didn't look like they were in good shape, so maybe they couldn't keep up.

Slowly, Edge gets back to his feet. "Okay, you kids stay right here with Hoppy. I'm going to backtrack and see if the clan caught them."

"What?" I gasp. "You can't leave us here." What if the clan didn't catch them and instead the Masons stumble across us?

"You'll be fine." Edge points to a thick clump of trees and bushes. "Hide in there. I'll be a lot quicker without you."

"No," Rocky says. "I'm going with you."

Beans pushes to his feet. "If he's going, then I am, too."

"Ditto." I nod.

Edge sighs. "Somebody needs to stay here in case Fynn and Scarlett got lost but find their way here. Rocky can go with me. You two stay."

Beans and I exchange a glower. I don't like this. I

want to go. They're my friends. But I guess it does make sense to stay here in case they find us.

"I can go," Beans says, straightening up like he's trying to be taller.

Edge cups him on the shoulder. "Thanks, but Rocky's bigger."

Beans presses his lips together and glances away, but Edge is right. If anyone can help, like in the strong way, it would be Rocky.

The two of them disappear back through the woods, and I turn to Beans. "Let's hide."

He doesn't say anything as he grabs Edge's pack and what meager things we managed to take back from the Masons and heads around a clump of bushes.

"Here, Hoppy," I quietly call as I follow Beans.

We get situated behind the bushes, and a lot of weird quiet seconds go by. It's Beans who speaks first. "We should've booby-trapped that moonshine barrel to explode."

I smile, glad he's not in a bad mood about the "Rocky is bigger" thing. "Absolutely not. Are you kidding me? They don't need any more reason to come after us."

Beans begins looking through the stuff we managed to grab, and my thoughts wander to the silo and the meteor shower. The bear and the river. The skeleton and our kidnappers. This isn't exactly how I thought things would go.

Hoppy nudges my elbow with his wet nose, like he's picked up on the tenseness, and I reach over and scratch his scraggly head. "You're a good boy," I tell him, and his tail wags. I love dogs. Maybe I should've asked for one for my birthday instead of a boom box.

Beans opens Edge's pack next, and I say, "You shouldn't do that."

He ignores me, finds a pad and pencil, and goes about sketching. Curious, I watch him for a few seconds and then lean in to see. He turns his back to me, hunching his shoulders and not letting me look.

God, what is his problem? Ugh.

A couple of minutes go by, and idly I listen to the scratch of pencil across paper. To the wind blowing leaves around. To something, probably a squirrel, scurrying past. I wonder if Edge and Rocky have made it back to the clan's camp yet. A mosquito lands on my arm and I smack it.

"Shouldn't they be back by now?" I ask.

Beans ignores me.

With a sigh, I look around and my gaze lands on a huge maple tree a few yards away. It reminds me of that one last year we all jumped from. Well, all of us except for Beans…

I finished raking our yard and leaned against a tree, studying the big pile of leaves.

The Scouts wandered up. "Whatcha doing?"

"Thinking about jumping. From there." I looked up at the treetop, then down to the leaves. "To there."

Beans took a step back. "I don't know. The weight-to-distance ratio seems off."

We ignored him and climbed to the top.

"Suppose we'll break any bones?" Fynn asked as we inched out on a limb.

"Nah," Rocky said.

We all jumped together.

"OWWW!"

"I told you so!" Beans yelled.

The scratch of pencil gets a little quicker, bringing me from the memory, and I crane my neck to see over Beans's shoulder. It looks like he's re-creating the map. I study the back of his bent head and automatically reach up to remove a little leaf stuck in his curls. He doesn't notice. Or if he does, he ignores me.

I chew my thumbnail, but it's already down to the

quick, so I try my middle finger. Edge and Rocky should be back by now. I stop nibbling and strain to listen for the sound of footsteps, but I can't hear anything. What if they got captured? What if a bear got them? What if—

Then it hits me. The fault. It's all on me. I'm to blame. I'm the one who insisted we go on this crazy adventure. My friends are lost in the woods, being chased by some kind of crazy kid murderers, and if anything happens to them, it will be my fault.

"We need to go home," I say. "I'm not sure this is going to work."

Beans turns to look at me, but he doesn't say anything, and I can't really figure out what he's thinking.

"Beans," I softly say. "We were just kidnapped and now Fynn and Scarlett are missing. And what if Rocky can't find them? What if they don't come back? Plus, we need to tell someone about Basinger."

"I don't want to quit," he says. "Please, Annie."

"Beans, we'll find another way to save your house."

"This is it, Annie. This is it. You were right. The meteor, it's the solution. I know it."

I look into his worried eyes, and the more I do, the more I imagine life without Beans. No, he can't move away. I'll do whatever I can to help him. "Then will you please tell Rocky and Fynn?"

He looks away—in embarrassment or in guilt, I don't know—but I stare at the side of his face for a couple of long seconds, and I don't get it. Why doesn't he want to tell them what's going on?

A twig snaps, and Beans and I fall even quieter. I reach for Hoppy and silently pull him against me. Another twig breaks, and our eyes go wide. Someone is definitely out there.

"Forget your friends," Scarlett gripes. "I want to go home."

"You're such a baby," Fynn snaps.

"Fynn!" I scramble out from behind the bushes and throw my arms around his shoulders. "You're okay!"

He gives me a couple of awkward pats. "Uh, yeah."

I let go of him and have this weird urge to give his cheek a big sloppy kiss. Fynn's here! And he's alive!

He looks around the area. "Where's everybody else?"

Beans comes out from our hiding spot. "Rocky and Edge went back to the clan's campsite to see if you were there. What happened to you two?"

Fynn shoots Scarlett an angry glare. "She tripped,

and I went back to help her, and by the time I got her up, you guys were gone."

"It wasn't my fault. You're the one who"—she wheezes mockingly—"couldn't breathe or run, even, with those stupid loafers."

Fynn shrugs. "At least I'm not a liar."

"I hate you!" Scarlett shouts. "You are the worst cousin ever!"

"Would you guys quiet down?" Edge steps through the woods with Rocky right behind him, takes one look at Scarlett and Fynn, and rolls his eyes. "What happened to you two?"

Fynn and Scarlett start yelling over each other, and I yell even louder. "Stop!"

Scarlett crosses her arms over her chest. "I want to go home. We all need to go home."

Rocky moves a little closer to her, and I swear he's about to put his arm around her again. "She's got a point. The Masons are on the move, too. If we keep going, we're going to run into them again."

"What happened when you guys went back?" I ask.

"We made it to the campsite and they were looking at the map," Rocky says. "We couldn't hear much of what they were saying, but I'm willing to bet they'll be going after the meteor."

"Which also means we need to get going if we're going to beat them to it," Beans says.

Scarlett throws her hands up. "Are you all insane? I'm not going anywhere except home."

"Can you not do anything other than be a pain?" I snap at her.

Then Rocky starts in on Beans.

Beans starts in on Fynn.

Fynn starts in on me.

And I turn to start back in on Scarlett when I realize one of us has to be "the voice of reason" (to use my mom's term). I'm used to settling all the Scouts' arguments anyway and so I hold my hands up, but of course no one gets quiet. I don't know why that gesture—holding hands up—works in the movies.

"Listen," I yell over everyone. "It's just a little farther. Did we really come all this way for nothing?"

Scarlett gets up in my face. "This is all your fault!"

I resist the urge to shove her away and I turn to Beans for help, but he's glowering at Rocky as Fynn starts yelling in Beans's ear.

What's happening to the Scouts?

A whistle pierces the air, and everyone falls quiet. Dang, I need to learn how to do that.

Edge holds his hands up, just like I did, but it works

for him. Well, maybe it was the whistle. "Do you want the Masons to find us?"

Silently, we all shake our heads.

"We don't have time to be goofing off like this," he declares. "Show of hands, who's got enough guts to go find the meteor?"

CHAPTER 12

Beans immediately throws his hand up, and I do, too. I look at the others.

With a sigh, Rocky raises his hand. "Oh, why not."

We all look pointedly at Fynn, and he does the only thing he can—he grudgingly puts his hand up as well. We look at Scarlett next, and she merely huffs with both hands firmly down.

Edge nods. "That settles it. Majority wins. We're going forward."

"But what about the map?" Scarlett whines. "We won't even know where we're going."

Beans holds up the new map he created. "We have our own right here."

Edge holds out his hand. "Why don't you give it to me? I know this area better than y'all."

"No way." Beans pulls back. "This isn't leaving my hands."

"Fair enough." Edge smiles a little. "But can I just see it real quick?"

Shaking his head, Beans turns the sketch against his chest. "I think you need to answer some questions first."

For whatever reason, Edge looks at me, and I shrug. "We don't even know you. So if you're coming with us, you better answer our questions."

"Okay." Edge gives us all an amused look. "Like what?"

"Like what are you doing out here in the woods?" Beans asks.

"Tracking the meteor like y'all. I saw it go down last night. But I was sitting on the front porch and didn't really see where." He gestures at the map. "Looks like you kids know."

Beans gives one single nod. "We do."

"How old are you?" I ask next because Beans really does have a point. This guy could be a serial killer. Okay, maybe not that. But still.

"Sixteen."

"Where do you live?" Fynn asks.

"In Friendly, Tennessee. Same as you, I suppose."

Rocky folds his arms. "Which high school do you go to?"

"Cherokee."

Rocky quickly follows that up with another question: "Do you play football?" I wonder what that has to do with anything.

"No, but I play baseball."

Beans gives Edge a long survey. "What do you want with the meteor?"

"Nothing. Just to see it. Maybe take a chunk of it as a souvenir."

"Do you have a girlfriend?" Scarlett asks, and every single one of us rolls our eyes. I guess she's feeling a little better about going on with the search.

Edge laughs. "No." He motions to the sketch. "Now can I see it? I just rescued you from the Masons. I'm not the bad guy here."

"Yeah, I guess he's okay." Beans turns the sketch around for Edge to look at.

Leaning in, he gives it a good solid study. "That's a few more hours of walking," he tells us.

"Listen," Fynn says. "We know the Masons are going after it, but if Edge saw it go down and we did, too, you know other people probably did."

Suddenly I remember what I overheard from our jail cell. "Mary Jo did say 'others' were after it."

Edge nods to the pile of stuff we left hidden behind the bushes. "Then let's get our stuff and get out of here."

Beans looks at Edge. "But just because you're older doesn't mean you're in charge or anything."

Edge laughs, and I think it's about the best one I've ever heard. All fun and chuckly and deep.

After that, we go about packing what items we managed to snatch from the Mason Clan. At this point we have three flashlights, Beans's new map, one walkie-talkie, Fynn's inhaler, some moist matches, the bag of pork rinds Junior had, and a pack of baby wipes that Fynn eagerly uses to clean his hands and face. I want to ask who brought the baby wipes, but of course I already know the answer.

I glance through everything one more time. "Did anyone happen to get my pocketknife?"

They shake their heads, and I drop my shoulders in disappointment. Yeah, my dad's really going to be upset at me over this one.

We divide up the pork rinds and each cram a handful into our mouths. I don't know who thought to grab them, but thank God. Edge passes around a canteen he had in his pack, but there's only enough water for a few gulps each.

After that, we fall in step behind Edge and Hoppy, and several minutes pass. The air feels hot and sticky now, and I try not to focus on how thirsty I still am. Hungry, too. I look around. Someone has to have more food.

Scarlett pulls a tube of lip gloss from her pocket and swipes it across her bottom lip. She rubs her lips together, and I look at how shiny they are and wonder what my lips would look like with that stuff. I watch as she hurries to catch up to Edge and immediately begins giggling at whatever he's saying. Edge smiles, and she giggles some more and my teeth clench. She said this was all my fault, and Beans just stood there and let her. Okay, I get that he doesn't want to tell anybody his secret, but he could, at the minimum, back me up.

With that irritable thought, I rear back and kick a rock, and it accidentally hits Scarlett in her calf.

"Ow!" She spins around.

"Sorry," I mumble.

She gives me a good solid glare that I ignore, before turning a smile back on Edge. "So," she says, all sweet-tempered again. "How'd your dog lose his leg?"

"Born that way," Edge tells her, and I find that comforting. I'd hate to think the little guy was in an accident or something.

"One of my good friends has a dog with only one leg," Scarlett says.

Edge's brows go up. "Really?"

She nods. "Swear to God."

I cut my eyes over to Fynn and he just shakes his head. I notice Hoppy is sticking close to Fynn. That's funny—Fynn doesn't even like animals. I watch as he dips his hand into his pocket and quickly drops a bit of something on the ground. Hoppy pauses to snatch it up and then goes right back to trotting alongside Fynn.

"Hey," I whisper. "Do you have more food? I'm starving."

Fynn looks at me. "No."

"But I just saw—"

"It's just a little bit of beef jerky I brought. It fell in the dirt, and since I wasn't going to eat it, I figured he might want it."

I look down at Hoppy gazing adoringly up at Fynn.

"I think you made a friend." And hello, Fynn's carrying beef jerky in his pocket? This is a first.

Edge looks over his shoulder at all of us. "Do your parents even know that you're out here?"

We shrug, and I'm the one who answers. "As long as we stick together, they're cool. We're always off doing something." That much is true.

"Yeah, well, how much trouble will you be in when you get back?"

I shrug, even though worry niggles through my belly. "They think we're on a camping trip, so they might not notice we're gone."

Scarlett grabs Edge's hand and tugs his attention back onto her. "We found a skeleton in a cave."

"We think it's Old Man Basinger," Beans tells him.

"No way." Edge thinks about that a second. "I saw him... well, come to think of it, it has been a while since I've seen him. You guys are going to tell someone, right?"

"Of course we're going to report it." Anonymously, but yeah, it's not like we're just going to leave a skeleton in a cave. Plus, we need to let the cops know we found Basinger's shotgun in the Masons' shed.

Edge stops walking, like he suddenly just thought of something, and turns to face all of us. "Wait a minute. A skeleton. In a cave. You didn't touch it, did you?"

"Maybe," Fynn says. "Why?"

Edge looks between us. "Obviously, you've never heard about the curse."

"What curse?" I hesitantly ask, ignoring the sudden chill pricking across my skin.

"Those caves were used as a burial ground by mountain witches. To keep anyone from trying to steal their gold, they put a curse on the chamber. Anyone who stole from it would be struck down and their skin would boil off. I wonder if that's what happened to Old Man Basinger? Oh, but you know what else? I heard that if someone touches a dead man's bones, they'll be cursed, too."

CHAPTER 13

Edge looks at all of us again. "You didn't touch the bones, did you?" This time he asks a little more emphatically.

Frantically, I search my brain. "I...I...I don't know. I think just the hat?" I turn to Beans. "Right? The hat?"

Beans shrugs. "I don't know. I didn't see."

Edge pats my shoulder and smiles at my panic. "I'm sure you're okay. Your skin is still on you." Then Edge turns and starts walking again, like he didn't just drop the bomb that I might be cursed.

Beans shakes his head. "There's no such thing as curses. Plus, we saw Basinger's shotgun in the shed, remember? If that was his skeleton, the Masons have got to be connected. Basinger wasn't stealing from some witch's chamber and then got cursed."

With that, Beans and everyone else follow Edge, and I just stand for a few seconds staring after them.

I didn't touch the bones. Did I?

I look down at the skin on my arms, and it looks normal to me. I give it a good hard rub just in case. He doesn't know what he's talking about. I hurry to catch up with the group.

"You don't think those Mason people will come back?" Scarlett asks several minutes later.

Edge shakes his head. "I think they're more interested in that map than anything. I've actually encountered the Mason Clan a few times. They're bullies, for sure, but as long as you don't mess with their moonshine, you're fine."

"Good thing I didn't booby-trap it, then," Beans mutters.

"Good thing," I say.

Edge steps around a tree. "It's weird they took you guys. Maybe they just wanted to mess with you. Scare you or something. I know the rumors, but I've never heard of them actually kidnapping anybody."

I remember the Masons standing side by side, staring at me hanging in that sack while I blubbered away. Maybe they realized they were overdoing the terrorize-the-kid thing.

Scarlett slips her hand in Edge's. "So you're in high school, huh?"

"Yep," he answers, sliding his hand free.

"I'm thirteen."

Edge gives her a lopsided smile. "Um, okay."

"What's so special about him?" Rocky grumbles.

"What's so special about Scarlett?" I grumble right back.

And when did I become such a girl? Thinking boys are cute, getting jealous, and the whole butterfly thing. Ugh. It's all Scarlett's fault.

Rocky cuts me an odd look through the side of his eyes, and I wish I hadn't said that about her out loud.

I decide to go with it. "Well?"

He shrugs. "She's different. New."

"Pretty?"

His face gets a little red. "Yes."

"She wears girly clothes and lip gloss?"

"Yes." He looks at me again. "What's up with you?"

I flip a braid over my shoulder. "So if I wore girly clothes and lip gloss, you would think I was pretty, too?"

Rocky doesn't answer me, and the more silence that ticks by, the more uncomfortable I become. What was I thinking, bringing this up?

"I don't know. I haven't really thought about it. You're just Annie to me. Always have been. You're my pal."

Well, I suppose there could be worse things than being Rocky's pal. Honestly, none of this has ever been an issue before and I'd really like it not to be. I smile at him. "You're my pal, too."

"Good." Rocky keeps walking, and when he's steps ahead, Beans comes up beside me.

"I think you're pretty," he quietly says.

For a second I'm not sure how to respond—Beans has never said anything like that to me before. I glance over at his face, and the shy expression on it melts my heart. "Thank you, Beans."

He smiles. "You're welcome."

Rocky stops walking. "Huh."

Beans and I jog to catch up, and when we're right beside him, we see him staring down at his Nikes.

He scoots away some leaves that are coated with a fine silver dust and then toes a fallen limb to the side. "What is that?" he asks.

I move closer, squatting as I do. And there, right at Rocky's feet, sits a perfectly round bright silver sphere, about the size of those Rubik's Cubes our math teacher lets us play with on Friday afternoons. Silver dust coats the ground around the sphere, too. This is just like the other silver powder I've seen. It had to have come from the meteor shower. I lean closer and reach out my hand—

"Don't touch it!" Edge says, and I jump back.

Rocky steps away, and Edge takes a stick and rolls the object around in the dirt and leaves.

"That silver stuff," I tell everyone, "it's been other places, too. It was on me and Beans and probably you all after the silo. It was on that bear. And on the Masons' roof. It's got to be from the meteor shower."

Fynn hikes one brow. "Why didn't you tell us you saw silver stuff?"

I give him an incredulous look. "We've been kind of busy. Excuse me for not pointing out sparkly glitter."

Beans straightens up. "She told me," he says, and Fynn and Rocky both frown.

I give Beans a look. Now is so not the time to be playing the favorite game.

The clouds shift then, and a beam of sun sneaks through them and the trees to hit the sphere, almost like the sun knows there's a foreign object in the woods. The sphere reflects back, shooting brilliant rays that are so bright I have to squint to watch. The rays seem to dance across the silver surface, and I'm suddenly mesmerized by the glimmering light. I reach a hand out again because I would love to feel—

"Don't." Fynn grasps my arm and tugs me back, and it's only now that I realize my friends have all taken giant steps back while I've moved forward.

The sun disappears behind a cloud, and the sphere goes back to being normal polished silver. What the heck just happened? I've seen the sun reflect on something shiny before, but this seemed different. More sparkly, and dancing with intensity. If this sphere came down in the meteor shower, then that means it's from outer space. I've seen pictures of meteors, and they never looked like this.

I glance at Beans. I want to know what he thinks. But he's just staring at the orb, and I can totally visualize the scientific wheels cranking away. Plus, this means more money.

Edge slips on a leather glove and reaches down to grasp the sphere. Holding it up in front of his face, he rotates the ball, studying it, and I try to get a better look. It almost seems like it's glass, it's so polished and clear. Edge pulls a handkerchief from his back pocket, wraps the cloth neatly around the sphere, and tucks the bundle inside his pack.

"What do you think it is?" Rocky whispers.

None of us have a response.

"This isn't what we're looking for, is it?" Fynn asks.

Beans shakes his head. "Wrong location. But, guys, what if what we saw really wasn't a meteor shower?"

"I told you..." Fynn's voice trails off.

"Aliens," Scarlett breathes.

CHAPTER 14

The word *alien* totally consumes me for the next thirty minutes. Gigantic ones with gray skin and misshapen heads. Little green ones with squeaky voices and bugged-out eyes. Tall, impossibly skinny ones with jagged teeth.

Swallowing, I glance over to Fynn, the one who initially planted the alien idea. I look at his blond curls, his dirty polo, and the side of his calm face as he merrily strolls along.

He doesn't seem fazed at all that we might be tracking an alien. Then again, he's always the one who plants these crazy supernatural ideas in our heads....

Fynn stuck his face in mine. "I heard she's a vampire," he whispered. And without moving his head, he rolled his green eyes to the left, across the field to where our gym teacher stood.

I rolled my eyes in the same direction, and my brain began to spin with ways not to get bitten.

Fynn dug around in his backpack and pulled out three necklaces chunked with raw garlic. He handed one to me. "Here, put this on."

Crinkling my nose, I put the necklace on and he did the same. "And the third necklace?"

Fynn looked grim. "You distract her and I'll sling it over her head."

I nodded. "I'm going in."

Yeah, Fynn's always the one bringing up this kind of stuff. Like that time he convinced us that werewolves had moved into our neighborhood. Don't even get me started with how much trouble we got in over that one—sneaking over to the new neighbors' house on the first full moon and hanging mistletoe from every tree in their yard and on their front porch, too.

Mistletoe's supposed to weaken a werewolf—at least that's what Fynn said.

With a sigh, he glances over to me now. "My feet hurt."

Rocky pipes up from the back of the group. "Of course your feet hurt. Who wears penny loafers to go hiking?"

Fynn spins to face him. "At least I have style! All you ever wear are jeans and muscle tees."

"You know what—" Rocky takes a step toward him. "You—"

"*And* you stink!"

Rocky hesitates a second, thrown off by the comment. "Yeah? Well, you do, too!"

"I do not!" Fynn lifts his arm and smells his pit. "Um, okay, maybe I do. But my Old Spice is back there with Mary Jo and Otis. I can't help that I stink."

I try to whistle like Edge did, but I end up spitting more than anything. So I hold my hands up instead, even though that didn't work before. Fynn and Rocky just keep arguing.

"Oh, would you two shut up," I snap. "We all stink. Just don't go smelling each other and we'll be good."

Scarlett giggles, and we all scowl at her. "What's so funny?"

She grins. "I was just imagining them as stepbrothers and sharing a room."

Rocky and Fynn both get real quiet. I look at Rocky first to see his jaw moving into a hard clench, and then I look at Fynn to see his facial expression slowly going from annoyed to smiling.

"Hey," Fynn says, "do you think we'll live at your house or mine? Come to think of it, either house we'll have to share a room. That is, until your sister goes off to college and then one of us can have hers."

The muscles in Rocky's jaw tighten even harder. "I'm not sharing a room with you."

Fynn's smile fades. "What's your problem?"

"My *problem*"—Rocky grinds out the words—"is that I don't want our parents getting married. I don't want to be your brother. What don't you get about that?"

I suck in a breath, Beans cringes, and Fynn's eyes narrow. "Oh, yeah? Well, I don't want to be your brother, either."

"Fine!"

"Fine!"

They stand there for a few seconds, fuming at each other, and it's Rocky who turns away first and charges off.

"Oh, my God," Scarlett says. "That was so mean."

I wish Fynn could see what's really going on with

Rocky. "Hey," I quietly say to Fynn. "He didn't really mean all that. I think this is more about his mom than anything. I think—"

"Why do you always take everyone else's side?" Fynn snaps, turning on me now.

My jaw drops open. "I don't always take their side."

"You do, too, and I'm sick of it." With that, Fynn charges off, just like Rocky did, and Scarlett hurries after him.

I stay right where I am, unable to comprehend what just happened.

Beans motions ahead. "Forget about it. Let's go."

I jab my finger at Fynn's retreating back. "Did you hear what he said?"

"Yeah." Beans shrugs. "It's kind of true, though."

"What?" I turn to face Beans. "It is not."

I frown. Is it?

Quickly, my brain spirals through all the disagreements we've had over the past year or so. Rocky and Fynn fighting over *Frogger*, Fynn and Beans arguing over homework, Rocky and Fynn disagreeing about how to roast a hot dog, Fynn and Beans yelling at each other about Halloween costumes...

Fynn's right—every single time I did take either Rocky's or Beans's side against his. And that was just this past year. Imagine all the times before that. I never realized I did that until this very second.

"Come on." Beans gives my arm a tug. "Let Rocky and Fynn figure out their parent issues. Just stay out of it."

With a nod, I slowly start to follow. I know Rocky and Fynn don't need me to settle their argument, but still this whole thing stinks. I don't want to stay out of it, especially after what Fynn just said. Now I kind of want to settle their argument, to take Fynn's side just to show him I can.

And to think I thought this trip would be good for them. For all of us. It seems to be anything but. They've all got other friends, and now all we do is argue. My stomach drops on a new and horrible thought. What if, after this, none of us want anything to do with one another anymore? What if the Scouts won't exist by the time this is over? What if I'm losing my best friends and I didn't even realize it?

A couple of minutes go by while I keep walking and staring at Fynn's back, and all I can do now is think about all the arguments where I never once took Fynn's side. Why is that? I like Fynn a lot, so it has nothing to do with that. Maybe it's because Fynn sometimes gets a little mean, like he did back at camp when he mentioned Beans's big allowance. Though it's not like Fynn intends to hurt people's feelings—it just happens.

Or maybe I take everyone else's side because Fynn always seems so sure of himself. Or because he's a good talker. Or because he gets so much attention in school because of his looks, and I feel like if I take Beans's or Rocky's side, it'll show Fynn he's not always the best, he's just a normal kid, like us.

I was purposefully messing with his confidence, and that makes me a horrible friend.

"You don't think it's an alien, do you?" Beans asks.

"Huh?"

"The silver ball."

"Oh. Do you?"

He hesitates a second before shaking his head. "Nah, guess not."

I glance ahead to where Edge and Scarlett are walking and talking. Or rather, she's talking and he's politely nodding. I take in his backpack and think of the way he reacted when we found that silver thing. Almost like he knew in advance not to touch it.

Leaning into Beans, I whisper, "What do you really think it is?"

His eyes narrow, like he's been pondering that

question the whole time I've been thinking about Fynn. "I don't know, but I would be incredibly curious to break it open and find out."

I like the sound of that. "How would we break it open?"

"The seam. If we could wedge a knife or something into it."

"There was a seam?"

Beans's eyes brighten with excitement. "Oh, yeah. It's the first thing I noticed."

I look at Edge's backpack again, formulating a plan to get into it, and my eyes lift to see him glancing over his shoulder at me. He smiles, and all kinds of butterflies dance through me. Quickly, I look away, my face so hot I know it has to be red.

The trees open to a field covered in at least an acre of tall sugarcane stalks. So tall, they tower above everyone's head, including Edge's. Automatically, I lift up on my toes but of course don't see any better.

Beans unfolds the sketched map and gives it a long look. "Wish I had my compass," he mutters.

"Here." Edge tosses him one. "Use mine."

"Thanks." Beans studies the map and the compass for a few seconds. "Yep. We gotta go straight through this field. We can go around, but that'll double our time."

"And you're sure about that map?" Edge questions.

Beans smirks. "I'm sure. Wish one of us was tall enough to see the other side of this field, though."

Edge looks at all of us and then his eyes land on me. "You're the smallest." Taking off his backpack, he gets down onto his knees. "Climb up on my shoulders. Between the two of us, you should be able to see the other side."

I don't immediately move. Climb up on his shoulders? That means I'll be touching him.

Scarlett pushes past me, fluffing her blond hair as she does. "I'll do it."

Edge's lips quirk into this puzzled smile, like he has no clue why I'm frozen. I watch as Scarlett wraps her spandex-covered legs around his neck and he lifts her up high.

She gives a little squeal that snaps me out of my nervous haze, and I scowl up at her. Hey, that's supposed to be me up there!

Squinting, she peers out across the field of sugarcane. "I see the other side. But it's a really long way. I can't see anything to the right or left."

Edge lowers her back down, and she takes a bit too much time climbing off.

"Well, all right, then." He picks up Hoppy and starts off through the towering stalks. "Here we go."

We fall into a sort of hodgepodge clump, with Edge leading the way and all of us using our arms to move green and brown stalks and leaves aside, making our way through the field.

"Ow!" says Fynn.

Over his shoulder Rocky shoots him a look. "Well, don't walk behind me if you don't want to get hit."

Fynn flips him off, Rocky ignores it, and I sigh.

Scarlett cringes. "Ugh. This is awful."

"How much farther?" Beans asks.

Why is he asking that? He's the one with the compass.

"Ow!" This from Fynn again.

"Well, stop walking behind Rocky," I snap at Fynn before realizing I just took Rocky's side again.

Sigh. Okay, next time I'll take Fynn's.

A few more minutes go by, and I wipe a bead of sweat trailing down my neck.

Rocky turns to look behind us. I follow his gaze to see nothing but cane, and my nerves frazzle a little. I don't like that I can't see the other side. I don't like it at all. What if this is like one of those weird mazes and we never come out the other end? I really hope Beans knows what he's doing.

A shadow rolls by and dark clouds move in.

Beans nudges me, and I glance over to see him put his finger to his lips. He points over to the left, where—tucked between stalks and embedded in the ground—there lies another one of those silver balls, with matching dust glittering on the ground and on some of the surrounding stalks, too.

I nod for him to go get it while the others keep moving forward, and Beans tiptoes over to the left. This sphere is smaller than the first one, but just as bright and smooth and silver.

Beans takes his pack off and rummages inside. I glance quickly forward to see the back of Rocky. A few more steps and my friends will be out of sight. Back to Beans as he picks up the object with a pair of his underwear.

Gross!

He wraps the sphere and places it inside his back-pack and then makes his way back over to me.

"Um, underwear?" I ask.

He shrugs. "I saw that Edge didn't touch the first one, so I figured I'd better not touch this one."

"Yeah, but *underwear*?"

"What? They're clean."

"Annie!" Edge yells urgently. "Beans!"

"Coming!" we yell back, and take off in the direction we think their voices are coming from.

CHAPTER 15

Too many minutes later and after several rounds of Marco Polo, me and Beans finally catch up to the others.

And they're not happy.

In fact, all of them are giving us the same disciplinary faces that teachers tend to give.

"I'm sorry," I say. "We got sidetracked."

Edge turns around and stalks off. "Well, don't get sidetracked again."

I stick my tongue out at him and it makes me feel a little better. Though I don't like Edge being irritated with me. My friends being mad at me is one thing, but Edge—I don't know, it's different.

On we trudge through the field with Beans checking the compass every now and then. I don't know how much time passes, but it seems like ages.

"Are we sure we're doing okay?" I ask.

Edge pauses and glances over to Beans, who nods and says, "Lift Scarlett up to double-check."

Edge motions to Scarlett, and she happily goes right up onto his shoulders. I might have climbed up there this time if he'd asked.

"The other side's just over there." She peers straight ahead, then to the right, then behind us, and then to the left. "Oh, my God," she whispers, pushing at Edge's shoulders. "Let me down. Let me down!"

Immediately he does, and she scrambles to hide in the stalks, motioning us down, too. "Th-th-there are men," she whispers. "They're dressed in that military camo stuff." She points to the left. "That way. A whole group of them."

I give Beans a worried look.

"What are they doing?" Edge quietly asks.

"They're walking through the stalks just like us."

"They're after it, too," Beans says. "They're the 'others.' Whatever fell must be really important if the military's after it, too."

I think of the two silver balls we have. What will

the military do to us if they find out we have them? Do they even know about them? Do they know about the silver dust? Surely they have to. They're the military.

The area around us darkens, and I glance up to see more murky clouds drifting in, some even pitch-black. A cool breeze blows through the stalks, sifting them, and what's left of the sun completely disappears behind the mess in the sky.

Rocky gets to his feet. "We better go."

Sprinkles of rain begin to lightly splatter, and keeping low, we continue moving through the stalks. Just as we step free from the field of cane, a wild bolt of lightning tears through the sky, and we take off toward the woods in front of us. Thunder cracks the air around us, and we yell. With bad storms they say the heavens open and rain pours, and that is exactly what happens next.

"This way!" Edge yells over the storm, and sprints into the dark woods carrying Hoppy.

Rain saturates my sneakers, and I slip and slide and squish my way behind Edge. Thunder cracks louder than the first time and it propels me into a full sprint. Edge races up a hill, ducks beneath a clump of trees, and disappears into a big opening cut in the side of the hill. I don't think twice about following. Neither do the others.

We flick on the three flashlights we have left, and though I entered the opening bent over, I discover I can stand to my full height. In front of me, Edge has to stay hunched over, as do Rocky, Fynn, and Scarlett, but Beans and I can pretty much walk upright.

We stop to catch our breath. "Do you think they saw us?" I ask.

Edge shakes his head. "Doubt it. That storm's crazy. They're probably also running for cover. Let's get moving. I know where we're going."

We shuffle farther into the darkness and enter another cave. Actually—I glance around—we're in a big tunnel. About four feet wide and I'd say about as tall as Mom, and she's five three.

Beneath my soggy sneakers trickles a teeny-tiny trail of water. The walls aren't "live," to use Beans's term. No mud or softness. I reach out and touch them. They're hard and shiny and slick. Like black rock. Shale—that's what it is.

"What if they come this way?" Fynn asks.

Edge lets Hoppy down to walk beside us. "I don't think we need to worry. Unless you're a local, you don't know about these caves."

"Yeah, but if they're the military, they probably have satellite imaging and stuff," Beans says.

"Maybe. But the good news is that these caverns will keep us dry from the thunderstorm, and we'll still be heading in the direction of the meteor. Like I said, I know where we're going."

"You said 'good news.' What's the bad?" Fynn asks.

"Bats."

"What?" Scarlett yelps.

I spin my flashlight onto her at the same time Edge says, "Lower your voice."

"No." She shakes her head. "No." And starts backing away toward the entrance.

"Scarlett," Edge says again. "It's no big deal. Just keep your voice down."

She backs up some more, still shaking her head. Something behind her catches my attention. I flash my light and see the background more clearly. There's a fork. A second tunnel. The one on the right looks strange. Darker than the one on the left, which is the one we came through.

I reach for her. "Scarlett, stop."

"You can't make me!" She turns.

And she runs.

"Scarlett!" I yell as she takes the wrong fork. "Not that way!" But she disappears into the darkness.

I don't think twice as I take off after her.

"Annie!" my friends holler, and their voices echo through the tunnel.

My flashlight catches a hint of Scarlett's blond hair and I run faster. "Scarlett!"

Her hair vanishes, and what can only be described as a bloodcurdling scream rebounds back to me. My guts clench with utter fear. Then my toe catches on something, and I trip and roll, and suddenly I'm sliding down a black, muddy chute.

Terrifying darkness engulfs me, and my arms and legs flail to grab on to something. But I'm going too fast! And oh, my God, what's at the bottom? Sharp rocks? Hungry cave animals? *Water?* "NO-O-O!"

CHAPTER 16

I land hard on my feet, and the jarring ricochets through my bones. My feet slide out from under me, and I plunk down onto my butt straight into something thick and gunky. All the air leaves my lungs, and I gasp it right back in, realizing I'm alive. I'm alive!

I hear crying. Scarlett's somewhere nearby.

I blink. And I blink again. What happened to my flashlight?

It's black. So black—I hold my hand in front of my face—I can't even see my fingers. Blood races through my body, and the beat of my pulse throbs in my ears. My senses prick to high alert, and I yell, "Help!"

"I'm here." Scarlett whimpers. "Annie?"

I take a breath. And then another.

"Are you okay?" she whispers from my left.

I hear movement, and then her hand touches me, and we both scream before simultaneously reaching out. We cling to each other, crying, gasping for air. We're alone in the dark and we have no clue where we are. Where the others are. How to get out. What if there is no way out? What if we're going to die in this dark tunnel?

Minutes pass, and we both gradually go from crying to sniveling and gasping to breathing. Slowly, my racing pulse begins to thump steadily and deeply, and with it the realization that I'm not hurt.

I take a second and move my arms and my legs, then my hands and my feet. Yes, I'm okay.

Scarlett sniffs, and I don't bother hiding the irritation in my tone when I ask, "What were you thinking?"

"I'm sorry," she whispers. "I'm so sorry. I thought I was running back toward the entrance."

With a sigh, I push her away. "Just help me look for the flashlight. It had to have fallen with me."

Scarlett grabs on to me. "Please don't let go of me."

I stop feeling around for the light and look in her direction. "Scarlett, are you afraid of the dark?"

"Yes." She whimpers. "Please. Please don't let go of me."

Her pleading tone softens my temper, and I grab her hand. "Okay. I won't let go. Just start feeling around for the light."

She death-grips my hand back. "Okay. Okay."

For the next several minutes we crawl around in the dark and the mud. I don't even want to think about what I might be touching.

The boys—they're somewhere above us. I know that much. I can't hear them, but I know they're up there somewhere. I tell myself not to think about our situation because that's just scary. Too scary. What if we can't find the flashlight? What if we can't get out of here?

Should we scream and see if someone hears us?

But if we scream, it might wake up the bats. Or shake something loose. I once saw on TV how these people were caught in a cave and a loud noise made the cave crumble. Yeah, we both need to stay silent.

"Found it." Scarlett breathes a sigh of relief and immediately flicks on the light.

Black and white dots swim in my vision, and it takes a second for my eyes to adjust, but when they do, I blink hard and look around. We're in a small room about the size of my parents' master bathroom. Mud covers the walls, the ceiling, and the floor. The room is compact, and neither one of us can stand up in it. It's a good thing we were crawling and didn't try. We would've banged our heads.

Scarlett points the light up to where we both just came from—a narrow, muddy hole above our heads. I stare at the flashlight beam as it glows into the darkness, gradually blurring into nothing. There's really no telling how far down we slid. With all that mud, there's no way we're climbing back out.

She moves the light around the room, and straight across from where we sit is our way out—a hole, an opening in the wall.

Together we move toward it, crawling through the mud and gunk. Scarlett shines the light into the hole and I grimace.

There are worms. Everywhere. Short. Long. Fat. Skinny. Creeping all over one another. Completely covering the walls, the floor, and the ceiling of the crawl space.

"That is *so* nasty," she says.

I blow out a breath. "Good thing you're not Fynn.

He'd rather stay in this room and die of an infectious disease than crawl through that."

She looks over at me. "How far do you think it is?"

"I don't know. Let's just get in there and make it quick."

Scarlett nods. "You first."

CHAPTER 17

Me first. Of course.

Taking the flashlight from Scarlett, I stare down the length of the crawl space again as it glistens and creeps with worms. I turn to her. "Like I said—fast. Got it?"

She nods. "Got it."

I take a breath. "Okay, here goes."

Carefully, I climb up into the crawl space, and my fingers and knees immediately sink into mud and squirming worms. One plops onto my back, and I fight the urge to cringe.

Scarlett pushes my foot. "Go!"

I take off as fast as I can, holding the flashlight and shuffling through the muck. In my peripheral vision I see one particularly fat creature crawling down my shoulder.

"Oh." Scarlett moans. "Gross."

Faster I go, trying not to think about the fact we're slugging our way through worm poop, too. At least they're not spiders. Just the thought of that makes me shiver.

I hear Scarlett spit, and I immediately press my lips together. I'm not getting one of these things in my mouth!

The crawl space opens wide, and I slide out of it and onto a dirt floor. Scarlett plops down right beside me, and we both immediately jump to our feet. The flashlight beam bounces around as we hop and jump and sling worms off our bodies.

I grab one crawling up Scarlett's back and fling it aside. She slides one out of my back pocket and tosses it into the crawl space.

We look at each other... and burst out laughing. I have no clue what I look like, but I imagine it's just like her. Top to bottom muck.

She runs her hands down her arms and lobs off black ick. "I don't even want to know what's on me."

I laugh even harder. "I'd give anything to see Fynn do what we just did."

She chuckles. "He'd never make it."

"You're right about that." Still smiling, I flash the light around the room we're now in.

It's big, just like the one that had Basinger's skeleton, but empty. No stalagmites or stalactites. Nothing at all. Just a big dry room.

"I bet you hate that you're stuck with me," Scarlett mumbles.

The smile still lingering on my face falls away, and I turn to look at her. She's staring around the room, pretending like she didn't say what she just said. It reminds me of yesterday, when she commented on how great it must be to have such good friends.

And, like yesterday, guilt nestles in, and it mixes with pity.

She looks over at me and smiles a little, and I give her a playful shove. "I like being in here with you," I tell her, surprised to find myself actually meaning it.

She makes a face, and we both chuckle.

"Come on." I nod toward the center of the room. "Let's find a way out."

As we walk side by side, I start thinking about my friends. What if we don't get out? What if we can't find them? We're going to be in so much trouble. "Everyone was heading in the other direction, right?"

Scarlett stops and looks around. "Actually, we came down the chute and crawled through the hole." She points. "They should be above us somewhere in that direction." She grabs the light and shines it on another crawl space, this one smaller than the one with the worms. "There."

Together we get closer and survey the opening. It sits about three feet off the ground. No bugs. Nothing. Just a nice dry hole. But small. We'll have to crawl on our bellies.

She takes a deep breath. "I'll go first this time."

Into the hole she goes, and I follow. On our stomachs we slowly crawl, and the farther in we go, the smaller and smaller the hole becomes, until I'm not sure if we're going to be able to continue.

"Ravioli or spaghetti?" she asks.

"Huh?"

"I've got to think about something else or I'm going to claustrophobically freak out on you. So ravioli or spaghetti?"

"Ravioli."

"Gum or lollipops?"

"Gum."

"Pepperoni or cheese pizza?"

"Cheese."

"Coke or Pepsi?"

"Coke."

"Hamburgers or hot dogs?"

"Hot dogs."

"Have you ever kissed a boy?"

Rocky pops into my mind and my face heats up. Why would I think of him in the same sentence as kissing?

"Oh, my God!" Scarlett excitedly says. "You have, haven't you?"

"What? No. No!"

"Oh. Well, I have. His name was Scott. He tried to French me and I told him no."

"Scarlett, that's gross! I'm never letting a boy stick his tongue in my mouth."

She giggles. "I might if it were Edge. He's so phat."

Yes, he's definitely that. "Why have you been flirting with Rocky, then?" I mean, if she likes Edge, why bother with Rocky?

Scarlett doesn't answer, and just when I think she's not going to, she says, "I don't know. It's what I do. I flirt. I like it. It's fun."

I don't get it. What's so fun about all the weirdness? Heck, just the thought of flirting makes me a little queasy.

She continues. "Kind of like when I embellish stories. I like it when people notice me. It makes me feel good about myself. And also kind of crappy, I guess. I mean, I'd rather not tell lies, but they come out of my mouth before I know it. My counselor tells me I'm trying too hard to get people to like me."

"Your counselor?"

"When my parents got divorced, the court ordered all of us to see a counselor."

"Oh." That must stink, being ordered to see a counselor. And having your parents get divorced. I wonder what it would be like to only ever see my parents separately. "So the NASA telescope wasn't true?" Of course, Fynn already told me the answer, but I ask the question anyway.

"Oh, I made a telescope, that part's true, but no, not the NASA thing."

I wonder how many of her tales have some sort of truth to them. Like the squirrel. Maybe she really did get bitten and made up the rabies part. "You know, you don't have to do that around my friends. The embellish thing. Just be yourself. They'll either like you or they won't."

Though I'm behind her and can't see her face, I get the feeling she's smiling. "Yeah, I'm getting that. The problem is, like I said, the lies come out of my mouth before I even realize it."

"'Second nature.' That's what my mom calls it when you say or do something before thinking."

"Lying is 'second nature' to me." Scarlett thinks about that a second. "You're right, it is."

"'Something to work on.' That's something else Mom says. To find your weakness and work on it."

"Hmm. Come to think of it, I haven't embellished in a while. At least not around you all, but I did with Edge when I told him I had a friend with a one-legged dog. I think my counselor would still be proud, though. She'd also probably say my behavior is getting better because I'm getting comfortable with you and your friends."

"They're your friends, too, now."

"Yeah, I guess they are." Scarlett keeps moving forward. "Okay, then what's your weakness? What's your 'something to work on'? Other than swimming, of course."

I give that question some good solid thought, and I frown. "I have a lot. My room is always messy. I don't study. I give Mom a hard time about all the girly clothes she buys me, because I never want to wear them. Pretty much any time I sneak off with the Scouts, I fib about it. And...I'm really possessive of my friends." It's hard admitting that last one, but it's true. I like having them to myself, and I don't like that they're all making new friends outside of our group. "I suppose that makes me selfish."

"Nah—you've been pretty good about sharing them with me."

Not really. She just doesn't realize it. "I'll do better."

"There! We're here!" She crawls out of the hole and drops three feet down, and I fall right on top of her.

Straight into cold water.

Scarlett screams, and we pull each other to our feet to discover we're standing ankle deep in water. Scarlett flashes the light around a room that looks to be about as big as my school's gymnasium. Water fills the entire area. From one wall to the next and back.

I sigh. Why does it have to be water? I swear to God, if I make it home after all of this, I'm getting swimming lessons.

If I make it home? When did I start thinking that way? Please. I'm going to make it home. We all are.

We have to.

Scarlett hands the flashlight to me, and leaning down, she scoops up some water and starts cleaning off the mud caked on her body from the previous crawl space. As she does that, I run the light beam across the murky surface. I'm not sure she should be splashing herself with this water. "Um, is it just me, or does it seem like there's silver glowing in the water?"

She stops with her cleaning and together we study the water for a second, and sure enough—there are silver particles floating in it. I look around the room again. So does that mean one of those silver balls came this way? Or maybe the silver is here because it rained and the water flowed in here from up top.

Suddenly, the light bounces off something all the way on the other side of the room. "It's the next crawl space," I say.

Taking the light back, Scarlett studies the water again. "That's definitely silver."

"It's all connected to whatever fell from the sky."

She sucks in a breath. "You don't think there's an alien in here?"

I catch my own breath and look back down at the water. "Can aliens swim?"

"I-I don't think so."

But she doesn't sound very convincing.

We move closer to each other until we're touching.

I'm completely ready to dive back into the crawl space we just came from if need be. But there's nothing here. Just us and the water.

I hope.

"Okay," Scarlett says. "I say we stick to the wall. Water's only ankle deep. We'll just make our way around the room to the other side and get out of here."

Something brushes my leg, and I jump. "Did you feel that?"

She freezes. "What?"

I jump again. "That!"

She flashes the light straight down and we both leap back. Fish! Everywhere. Big ones! But there's something wrong with them.

Something scary.

These don't look like any fish I've ever seen. They're a grotesque milky white, like a foot long and just as wide, with no eyes.

We scream, and the fish scatter. I guess they can hear us.

I reach for Scarlett. She reaches for me. And we cling to each other as we hop from foot to foot.

"Whatarethey, whatarethey, whatarethey?" she chants.

"I don't know." I climb the three feet right back

into the hole we just came out of, and she scampers in after me.

Together we lie squished, our flashlight trained down into the water, staring wide-eyed, waiting for the fish to make another appearance.

Just when my pulse starts to calm back down, a few of them surface. I swallow, and the sound gurgles in our tiny space. Side by side we watch as the fish saunter by, lazily moving, out for a merry little stroll. Or rather, swim.

"They seem harmless," I say.

Scarlett nods. "Yeah, but they're ugly."

"I bet Beans would know what they are."

"Yeah, bet so."

A few baby ones float by, and I smile. "Those are cute."

"Why don't they have any eyes?"

I shrug. "Maybe it's a cave thing. They don't need them in the dark."

She takes a breath and looks over at me. "Well, what do you think?"

I think about a National Geographic video we saw at school about sharks. Not that these are sharks, but the film pops into my mind anyway. "No sudden movements. We'll make our way around the room, slow and steady. If they wanted to eat us, they would've already nibbled on our ankles."

"That's a good point." She nods. "Okay, I'll go first."

"That's brave of you."

Scarlett shrugs off that comment and out the hole she goes. I watch as the fish lazy on up, swim around her ankles, and head off.

I release a breath. Boy, she is brave.

"You coming?" she asks.

"Oh, sorry." I slide out and into the water and stand dead still while the fish do the same to me.

Once they finish inspecting and are gone again, Scarlett grabs my hand, and I grab hers back. "Okay, steady. Around the room we go."

She leads, and I follow. We keep our backs plastered to the cave wall and carefully shuffle our feet along the perimeter of the water-filled room. The fish come and go, but, truly, they are harmless. I can't wait to tell the boys about them.

"Uh-oh," she says.

"'Uh-oh'? What uh-oh?" I don't like uh-oh.

Scarlett takes a step down, and the water now hits at her knees. "A dip, but the gap is only a few feet. No big deal."

Gripping her hand, I step down, too, but my foot

slips and I fall straight into the water. It rushes into my mouth and I flail my arms—*no, not again!* I spit and swallow and spit some more, and suddenly I feel a yank and realize Scarlett is pulling me up out of the dip.

She gives me a hard shake. "Annie, stop fighting! I'm trying to rescue you."

It takes every ounce of control I have, but I manage to refocus my brain into getting up beside her. When my back is plastered to the wall and I'm standing once again in ankle-deep water, I look over at her, and I don't bother hiding both the fear and gratitude in my voice. "Thank you."

She smiles. "That's what friends are for." She grabs my hand and continues around the rest of the room, and I carefully follow.

That's what friends are for. Huh, what do you know? I do have a new friend in Scarlett.

We reach the next crawl space, and I go in first this time. It's the least I can do since she rescued me and all.

More mud, no worms. And a couple of minutes later we plunk out the other side.

"There they are!" Rocky shouts.

I glance up as the boys race toward us. If I had a

bag of confetti, I'd throw it in the air right now. Rocky lands on top of me and squeezes me so tight I squeak. Then Fynn. Then Beans. Then we're in a group hug with Scarlett and me squished in the center. I swear someone kisses me on the cheek. I wonder if it's Rocky.

"You two stink," Fynn says. "And you're probably contagious." But he hugs us hard anyway, apparently forgetting he's mad at me.

Edge chuckles. "All right. Break it up. This tunnel right here leads us out."

CHAPTER 18

While Scarlett details everything that happened to us, I listen, smiling, wondering if she realizes she's not embellishing one single thing.

When it's my turn to talk, I tell everyone about the silver we saw in the water. "I know it's weird, but doesn't it seem like the meteor left a trail for us to follow? Almost like it's wanting us to find it?" Okay, maybe I'm stretching things a bit, but my imagination is running a bit wacky.

The boys look at one another, grinning, and I immediately know something's up. Edge unzips his pack and pulls out a different handkerchief. He unfolds it, and inside sits another silver ball the same size as the one Beans and I found in the field.

My mouth drops open. "You found one in here, too?"

Beans eagerly nods. "Must've fallen through an opening or something. How many do you think there are?"

We all look at Edge, like he's supposed to know the answer to that, and he just shrugs. "No clue, but if we keep going, we'll probably find more."

Excitement squirms around inside me. Yes, how many more are there, and what are they all going to be worth when we sell them? But more importantly, what are they?

As we near the exit of the cave, we hear voices and duck back into the darkness.

"I dunno why yuns don't just do a fancy helicopter or somethin'." It's Otis's voice.

"Because, sir, we don't want to alert the locals. How many kids were there?" From the formal tone I assume he must be one of the military camo people. But why would they be talking to Otis Mason? Don't they realize he's bad?

"Let's see. Five 'round the same age and then an older one," Otis says. "And that map of theirs was heading west 'round 'nother mile or so. But they took off with it, so I couldn't tell ya for sure."

What a liar! He has the original map.

"And how was it they got away?" the military guy asks.

"Hit one of mine o'er the head," Otis says, and my mouth drops open. We did not!

After that there are a few beats of silence, and then their footsteps shuffle away.

In the shadows of the cave, I look at all my friends. They seem as shocked as I am. "Guys, we should go out there and rat the Masons out. We should tell them they kidnapped us. We should tell them about Basinger's skeleton!"

"If we do that," Fynn whispers, "then this whole thing is shot."

"I don't know what all is going on," Beans says. "But not only is Otis lying to him about us, he's also told him the wrong way."

"Well," Scarlett says. "If they're heading the wrong way, that's good for us, right?"

Edge shakes his head. "If Otis is leading them in the wrong direction, I bet you anything Mary Jo and their sons are going in the right direction."

I chew on my thumbnail a second. "Yeah, but they're the military. They're not brainless. And why would they be asking Otis for help?"

"Because he can show them the ins and outs of

these hills better than any technology," Rocky says, and we all nod. That does make sense.

I look at my friends again. We've been through a lot, but I notice that no one is mentioning going home. Not even Scarlett.

"What time is it?" Fynn asks. "I'm starving."

Beans checks his watch. "Four o'clock, and I'm starving, too. But we're almost there."

"Think about the enormous pizza we'll eat when all this is over," Rocky says, and we all groan.

Four o'clock on Saturday. Seems like it should be Sunday. It's hard to believe that at this time yesterday we were coming home from our last day of school.

"Let's do this," I say, motioning them on ahead.

Fynn nods. "If the military wants it, whatever fell must be awesome, and we will find it first. Let's go."

We take a second to peek out and make sure the coast is clear, before clearing the cave. I follow the others out into a now drizzling, sunshine-filled afternoon.

"So how much farther to the meteor?" I ask.

Beans checks the compass and the map. "Shouldn't be much farther." Beans looks around. "There're supposed to be railroad tracks around here, and they'll take us pretty much straight to it."

"Up there." Scarlett points, and sure enough, up the bank and through the trees I see the tracks. "But first I have to pee." She grabs my hand. "Come on."

I yank back. "What? I'm not going with you." I pee alone.

"Yes, you are. You're going to stand guard while I do my business. I'm not going to have a snake sneaking up on me or a bear or those mountain people." She yanks me harder. "So, yes, you're going with me."

She does have a point about the Mason Clan, so reluctantly I go and stand guard while she squats behind a bush and wipes with a leaf because, of course, her toilet paper got soaked.

When she's done I take a turn, and I have to admit it is nice to have someone watching out for snakes and bears while I pee. As much as I love the Scouts, I would never allow them to pee-guard me.

When we get back, the boys are arguing.

"Let me see the map," Fynn says.

"No," Beans snaps.

"What's the big deal?" Rocky reaches for it.

Beans steps back and his whole face clenches into an angry line. "It's my map. It's my meteor. You wouldn't even know where to go without me!" With that he stomps off.

Fynn looks at Rocky. Rocky looks at Fynn. Then they both look at me.

I don't know what I just missed, but I defend Beans anyway. "He's right. It's his map. Just leave him alone."

Fynn throws his hands up. "See, you defended Beans again."

"Against you *and* Rocky," I point out, and Fynn angrily folds his arms and looks away.

"It might be Beans's map, but it's not his meteor. What's his problem?" Rocky asks.

"Maybe you're his problem," Fynn says, and goes stomping off, too.

Rocky spins away and charges up the bank toward the railroad tracks, keeping distance between him and the rest of us.

For a few seconds, I stand here, shooting furious glares at both of their backs, and then my gaze drifts up to Beans and I notice he's fiddling with something in his backpack. Oh, that's right, the silver ball we found in the cane field. I almost forgot about it.

"Hey," I whisper, jogging to catch up with him. "What are you doing?"

He glances around to make sure everyone is a distance away before saying, "I really want to see what's in this thing." He's careful to keep the orb hidden inside his backpack while tinkering with it. We keep walking.

"Beans." I sigh. "No more secrets. You need to tell Rocky and Fynn about your house and about this sphere you're hiding."

Beans ignores me, and I watch as he fiddles with the seam of the ball, trying to pry it open with his fingernails. I wish I knew what was going on with him.

"Maybe you shouldn't touch it," I tell him. "You saw how Edge handled it with a glove."

"Maybe you should stop trying to tell me what to do."

I stop walking. "What did you just say? I'm doing everything I can to keep your secret and you're mouthing off at me?"

Edge passes by, giving us a strange look, and Beans stops fiddling with the silver ball. He slows his pace and I follow his lead, slowing mine. Then Scarlett goes by, totally ignoring us as she focuses on catching up with Edge.

As we step onto the railroad tracks, Beans grabs a rock from between the wood slats.

"Maybe we can try to break it open with this," he quietly says, and starts picking at the seam again while I silently watch.

"Beans." I try again. "We need to tell everyone what's going on."

"You know what?" He tosses the rock down. "I'll figure this out on my own." Then he zips his pack up, throws it over his shoulders, and silently walks off.

I stay back for a second, staring at everyone ahead walking the tracks. After finding one another in the cave, I thought we were doing okay again, but no one is talking. No one is laughing. No one is having fun. It's almost like... we're not even friends anymore.

What happened to the Scouts?

CHAPTER 19

Minutes go by as I trail behind everyone, shuffling my feet, wishing I could turn the clock back and not even suggest this stupid adventure. Eventually, the tracks curve and we follow them around until we come to a halt.

There's a trestle that stretches from where we are all the way over to the other side. And way down below flows a calm and wide river. Calm and wide. That means deep. Real deep.

Edge doesn't seem to pay any attention as he picks up Hoppy and begins across the trestle.

I don't move. Neither do my friends. "Um, Beans, was this on your map?" I ask.

He looks way down toward the water. "Huh."

"'Huh'?" I repeat, because that is not the word I want to hear right now.

Ignoring me, Beans looks to the right, where the river seems to stretch for eternity, curving through the valley, and then to the left, where it does the same. He looks straight across to the other side. Then he pulls out his map and ponders it. "This might be either the Hiwassee or the Ocoee."

Rocky heaves an agitated breath. "Really, you're giving us a river lesson right now?"

Slowly, Beans turns to fully face Rocky, and Beans's fingers curl to two tight fists around the map.

Rocky just looks at him. "What's your problem?"

Beans's jaw tightens. "What's. My. Problem?"

"Yeah." Rocky hikes his chin. "What's your problem?"

To Beans's credit, he doesn't back down. "You're my problem." He looks at Fynn. "So are you." Then he looks at me. "And you, too."

Fynn steps up. "What did I do?"

"Yeah," I say. "And what did I do?"

"Back off." Rocky turns on Fynn.

Fynn gets in Rocky's face. "No, you back off."

I step up. "Why don't you both back off?"

Beans shoves them. "Yeah, back off."

Fynn shoves Beans back. "What the hell? Get your hands off of me."

"You think I'm afraid of you?" Beans looks between Fynn and Rocky. "Either of you? So what if you're bigger? I can take either one of you."

Now it's Rocky's turn to shove them. "I'd like to see either one of you try to take me."

I want to shove somebody and so I shove all three of them, Fynn first, then Rocky, then Beans. If we're about to have this out, then I'm in this, too. "This whole trip was supposed to be awesome and all we've done is fight. You three have ruined everything!"

Fynn sticks his face right in mine. "Like you're so perfect!"

After that the insults start flying.

You're a hypochondriac!

Yeah, well, your breath stinks!

You're high maintenance!

Your loafers are stupid!

I hate your muscle shirt!

You always have the stupidest ideas!

I hate your high-waters!

On that last one, Beans screams and launches himself at Rocky at the same time Rocky takes a swing at Fynn, and I leap on top of all of them. We all go rolling across the tracks and down the embankment. Fists fly. Legs tangle. Cuss words bling into the air. I hear an "umph." And then an "ugh." A few more fists. Some kicks. Another roll.

Somewhere in my peripheral vision I see Scarlett shuffling her feet, watching us, like she wants to get in on the action, too. I nod at her, like we're in the WWF and can tap in, and she shakes her head and backs away.

Okay, then. Whatever.

I grab a handful of dirt, ready to grind it in Fynn's face, and he gets me first, smearing mud all down my cheek and neck. Rocky yanks on a handful of Beans's hair. I put Rocky in a headlock. And Beans kicks Fynn in the shin.

"What the hell?" Edge shouts.

Then Beans accidentally knees Rocky in his crotch, and the fight comes to a grinding halt. It's a silent rule—no one goes for the crotch.

Rocky rolls away from my headlock, cupping himself, groaning. My hands go over my mouth. Scarlett gasps. And Fynn holds up his hands in surrender.

"I'm sorry," Beans says meekly, and Rocky grimaces with another moan.

Scarlett comes rushing down the embankment to

our pile, and I take a second to survey the injuries. Other than Rocky's current situation, we all look fine. Dirty, but fine. Fynn's polo is, of course, still somehow tucked in. How he manages to do that, I don't know.

Rocky inhales a few deep breaths and blows them out. Then carefully, he pushes to a sitting position and looks right at Fynn, which surprises me—I thought Rocky would go after Beans for the whole crotch-kneeing thing.

"You okay?" Fynn asks, and Rocky nods.

No one says anything for a few seconds as we all watch Rocky and Fynn staring at each other. Something's about to go down. Or if it's not, then it needs to.

I fold my arms. "I think we all need to have a come-to-Jesus moment." I waggle my finger between Rocky and Fynn. "You two first." With that, I stare them down, waiting, because if they're not going to talk, I'm sure going to make them.

Of course they don't talk willingly, and Fynn's words come back to me about always taking Rocky's and Beans's side. Well, it's time for me to take Fynn's. I refold my arms and give Rocky my best glare. "Fynn would make the best brother ever. Why would you say such mean things to him?"

Fynn gives me a surprised look, and I keep right

on glaring at Rocky until Fynn speaks. "You really don't like that my mom and your dad are together?"

Rocky shakes his head. "No, I don't."

"Is it me?" Fynn asks.

"No." Rocky looks down at the ground. "It's just... I'm not ready to have a new mom."

Fynn thinks about that for a second. "I get that." A couple of more beats go by, and then Fynn gives a disappointed shrug. "I was kind of looking forward to having a dad who was around a lot. And a brother and a sister."

Lifting his head, Rocky silently stares at Fynn, and I can almost see Rocky's brain wrapping itself around Fynn's point of view. Fynn's an only child and has never really had a dad, and Rocky's just now fully getting that.

"I said I wasn't ready." Rocky's lips twitch up into a tiny smile. "Not that I'm still not ready. I'm getting used to the idea."

Fynn's lips twitch, too, but he shrugs again, this time in a more shy than disappointed way. "Besides, it's not like they've told us they're getting married. They may break up."

"Or they may not," Rocky says.

"Or they may not," Fynn agrees, and both of their smiles get a little bigger.

I grin, too, so glad my friends have finally made up.

Beans gets up, making a show of dusting himself off, acting all macho and nonchalant. "I kicked your butts."

Fynn and Rocky both snort.

I look right at Beans, done with his secret. He needs to come clean. He needs to get over whatever his issue is. "You tell them or I will."

Fynn and Rocky exchange a look. "Tell us what?"

Beans narrows his eyes at me, and I simply look back. "I'm serious," I say.

Beans throws his hands up. "Fine. We're losing our house. It's being foreclosed on. Dad and Mom went to court, *again*, and now the judge says Dad gets custody, and I'm pretty darn sure that means I'm moving to Knoxville."

Rocky straightens up. "What? How long have you known?"

"Not long."

"Why didn't you tell us?" Fynn asks, rolling over to his knees.

"Because..." Beans's shoulders drop on a sigh.

"It's embarrassing, I guess. Rocky's got a great dad and they do all this stuff together. Fynn's mom is so fun and always throwing parties. Annie's parents are still together and always taking Annie to cool places. And all my parents do is fight. You guys are all I have, and now I'm losing you."

"Are you kidding me?" Rocky says. "You're not losing us."

Fynn nods. "We're not the Scouts without you. We'll figure this out."

Rocky looks right at me. "And you knew about this?"

"I promised Beans I wouldn't tell."

"Don't be mad at Annie. It was her idea about the meteor. That if we found it, we could sell it and make some money and maybe then I can stay because my mom could stop the bank from foreclosing on the house."

"Hell, yeah, that's what we're doing." Rocky stands up. "We're finding this thing, and you're staying."

Fynn starts to climb the embankment back up to the tracks. "Let's go — we're wasting time."

I look over at Beans. "See?"

With a little smile, he rolls his eyes. "Okay, I should've told them sooner."

"That's right, you need to listen to me next time." I

pick the map up out of the dirt and hand it to Beans, and he gives me a playful poke as we head up the embankment to join the others.

As usual, it takes me to make everyone talk. Always has. And that thought makes me pause. I never realized it until right now, but I'm the one who keeps everyone together. I'm the link. I hang out with Rocky and play sports. With Fynn, I bake. Beans and I are always tinkering with his experiments. But come to think of it, none of them hang out unless I'm around.

I'm the one who plans things. I'm the one who calls everyone. If it weren't for me, I wonder if the three of them would even be friends. Because Rocky has his football pals. Fynn has his church group. Beans hangs out with his science club.

Other than them, I don't have anyone else. Maybe Mom's right. Maybe I do need to start making new friends.

Only problem is, I don't want to. I like the ones I have.

As I think that through, I nibble on my pinky nail and glance at Scarlett. Rewind to before this trip and there was no way I'd ever be friends with her, but now somehow I am. And it's not a bad thing. I'm okay with her now.

Who would've thought?

When we're all back on the tracks and approaching the trestle again, I begin to notice it—the silver. But it's not powdery like before—it's clumpy. Almost gel-like. Sticking to the tracks in some areas and hanging from the trestle in others. I suppose the rain probably made it do that.

"So who's to say whatever we're after didn't fall into the river?" Scarlett asks.

Good point.

Rocky steps onto the trestle. "Only one way to find out."

I look down into the wide, calm, deep river. I could stay here. The others could go over, yell back when they know something.

Rocky turns to me. "Okay, this is nothing like before. It's sturdy. And wide. You'll just put your foot on one track and then the next and then the next and before you know it, we'll be across."

"Just don't look at the water in between the tracks," Scarlett says, and I roll her a look.

Fynn sighs. "Scarlett, that's not helping."

"Is no one going to point out the obvious that this is a *train* trestle?" Beans asks. "What if a train comes by?"

Scarlett starts across. "Then we'll run. Come on, let's do this."

I watch her as she begins confidently crossing, and all kinds of envy swirl around inside me. Yeah, I'm definitely getting swimming lessons. I'm done with being scared of water. I try to make a joke. "Well, at least none of us are afraid of heights."

Rocky steps in front of me and slips my fingers through his belt loops. "Just follow me."

Tightly I grip the back of his jeans and stare at the Wrangler patch above his butt as he slowly begins across. I concentrate on even breaths. In. Out. In. And on matching my steps to Rocky's. Left. Right. Left. And even though I can see the river between the slats, I make my eyes stay on that Wrangler patch.

Just when my eyes start to drift down to his butt, Rocky asks, "How about a song?"

"O-okay," I say.

He clears his throat.

"Oh, I went to Cincinnati and I walked around the block,
and I walked right in to a doughnut shop,
and I picked up a doughnut right out of the grease,
and I handed the lady a five-cent piece.
She looked at the nickel,

and she looked at me.

She said, 'This nickel's no good to me.

There's a hole in the center and it runs right through.'

Says I, 'There's a hole in the doughnut, too.

Thanks for the doughnut—goodbye!'"

Everyone laughs, and I look up and past Rocky to realize we're almost halfway across. He doesn't do a silly song often, but I love when he does. His mom taught him a ton of songs, and they're fun.

I'm about to prod him for one more song when my feet begin to tingle. I start to ask if anyone else's are tingling, too, when Scarlett speaks up. "Do another!"

Rocky holds his hands up, like he's onstage, and deepens his voice. "Thank you, thank you very much. Just a quick break and I'll be right back."

I smile.

My gaze drifts down to the tracks and the water flowing really far beneath, and I feel my body sway at the same time I catch myself and miss a step. I gasp, and Rocky jerks.

"Annie!" Beans yells from behind me. "Pay attention."

I cringe. "Sorry. I thought I felt the track—" I don't finish that sentence because not only does the track start to vibrate, but the distinct sounds of a train's engine and chugging wheels echo in the distance.

My spine goes rigid.

Oh. My. God.

A train is on the tracks!

"I told you so!" Beans yells right as the train's horn blares.

CHAPTER 20

Rocky reaches back and grabs my hand, and we take off in a full sprint. I don't look down. I don't look behind. I don't look anywhere. I concentrate on gripping his hand, staring at his back, and moving my feet as fast as possible.

"Run!" Edge yells.

"We are!" Beans screams.

"Faster!" Fynn hollers.

Scarlett screeches.

The train honks.

And, panting, I lift my knees, right-left-right-left, running, clinging to Rocky, and I swear at one point I walk on air.

Beneath us the tracks violently vibrate, and the movement rebounds through my bones.

I trip as Rocky reaches the other side and dives left, taking me with him. We land right on top of Scarlett. Then Beans lands on top of us. Fynn rolls past. Edge grabs all of us and drags us away from the tracks right as the train reaches us.

Shaking, I cling to my friends and press my eyes closed. The horn honks again, and the wind smacks my hair and clothes against my body as the train zips past.

A good solid minute later it's finally gone, and Beans is the first to speak. "I think I'm deaf."

I tune in to my own ringing eardrums and think I might be, too.

Rocky disengages himself from all of us and jumps to his feet. "That was awesome!"

"Are you kidding me?" Scarlett sucks in a couple of deep breaths. "We could've died!"

Fynn jumps up, laughing, wheezing, laughing.

Then Edge gets in on it and the three of them just laugh and laugh. Scarlett and Beans and I slowly sit up, dazed, looking at one another, at them. I'm not sure why, but we too start laughing. Maybe the insanity of this adventure has turned us stark raving mad.

As our laughing dies down, we gradually begin to

realize there is silver all around us. On the ground. In our clothes. Smeared on the trees. It looks like jelly, though, like it did on the tracks, as if the rain mixed with it. Automatically, I scan the area for another ball.

Without saying a word, so does everyone else. It's like our brains are connected now. Silver gunk. Ball. Meteor. This way.

"Come on," Edge says, and we follow him away from the tracks, over a dirt mound, and down into the woods. "Pair up with someone and spread out. Yell if you find anything."

Beans grabs me. "I'm with Annie."

Scarlett goes with Edge, Rocky goes with Fynn, and I turn to Beans. "Where do you want to start?"

"Let's go this way," he whispers, and I wonder what he's up to. A few seconds later, he glances over our shoulders. "Okay, they're gone."

Crouching, he unzips his backpack, and I know what he wants to do. Anticipation tickles through me, and I watch him pull the silver ball out. He takes a rock and begins picking at the seam, just like he did before. I kneel down beside him and watch as he picks, picks, picks.

But nothing happens.

With a sigh he rotates the sphere a bit and tries another section. "Maybe this is titanium or something."

I reach for the orb. "Here, let me try."

Beans hands it to me, and as my fingers touch the ball, I pause. It's slick and cold and unlike anything I've ever touched before. Sort of polished and oiled and wet, yet not wet. "Weird."

"I know, right?"

I rotate it, studying the perfect silver finish. "I don't want to ruin it."

"I don't, either, but I'm dying to see what's in it."

The more I study it, the more unsure I become. "I don't know."

"What do you mean, you don't know?"

"Well, what if there's something in here that can hurt us?"

"Like what?" Beans stares at me a second. "Fynn got to you, didn't he?" He grabs the ball back. "There is no alien in here. A tiny weird thing won't jump out and climb up our noses."

Like Fynn, I've seen *Alien* and any other number of sci-fi movies. Honestly, I don't know if extraterrestrials exist or not.

"Okay," I say. "What if it's a bomb? What if we break this thing open and it explodes?"

Surprise flicks through Beans's eyes, and he looks back down at the ball. I can tell the idea of a bomb hadn't occurred to him. And now that he's thinking about that possibility, I'm convincing myself even more we shouldn't break open this thing.

"Maybe that's why Edge handled it with gloves," I tell him.

"Uh, Annie, I, uh, hadn't thought of that." Carefully, Beans lowers the ball to the ground and just as carefully takes his fingers off the sphere.

Side by side we stare down at the polished metal.

"So, what now?" I ask. "We can't just leave it here."

"Okay, give me a second."

I watch as Beans thinks for a few seconds.

"Okay—logic. We've tramped through woods and caves and picked at it with a rock. It's obviously sturdy. If it was going to explode, it already would've."

"Unless it's on a timer." Because on TV, bombs have timers.

Beans gives that a second of thought, and just as he's ready to say something, Scarlett's voice cuts through the air. "We found it!" she yells.

CHAPTER 21

With the ball stowed safely back in Beans's pack, we find Scarlett, Edge, and Hoppy standing in a small clearing covered in thick silver gunk that lies in these long streaklike fingers, almost like they're pointing at something. Black ash chars the ground and the surrounding trees, making it obvious that whatever landed here burned the terrain. Thank God it rained. This thing could've started a forest fire.

The long fingers lead straight toward a rectangular piece of rusted metal that lies on the ground. Actually—I realize as I get closer—it's a door with hinges and a latch, and there's a jagged hole right in the center about the size of a basketball.

That's weird. A door out in the middle of the woods? Why would there be a door out here?

Rocky comes sprinting through the trees from one direction and Fynn the other. Weren't they supposed to stay together?

We all stand for a second in the clearing and just stare.

It's Edge who speaks first. "Know what that is? That's a door leading to a storm shelter. There used to be a cabin here a long time ago. I bet anything there're supplies down there. Canned goods and whatnot."

I turn and survey the cleared area, and sure enough, I can visualize a little cabin right here with all these woods surrounding it. Secluded. Like where some mountain man might have lived once upon a time.

Edge leans down and grabs the handle and creaks open the door all the way, letting it rest on the ground. Simultaneously we take a step closer and lean in. A few wooden steps lead down and gradually disappear into the darkness. There's no telling what's down there.

With that thought, I back up a little.

Rocky squats next to the door and runs his fingers

around the basketball-size hole. "This looks new. Check it out—it's not rusted or anything."

Beans does his scientific thing, leaning in, studying the hole in the door. I swear if he had a calculator and a protractor, he'd probably whip those out, too. "Whatever fell shot right through."

"What if it's the alien?" Fynn whispers.

I swallow. Good point.

For a few seconds, no one speaks, and then Beans looks around the area. "Everyone find a weapon."

We all scramble away, coming back seconds later with various things—a stick, a rock, a broken Coke bottle. I look at the broken bottle in Fynn's hand. "Where'd you get that?"

He nods over his shoulder. "In the woods. It was the only one."

Beans flips on his flashlight. "Ready?"

I crowd in behind him. "You're going first? You're so brave."

As usual, Rocky steps up. "I'll go first."

Beans straightens his shoulders. "I got this."

Holding both hands up, Rocky backs away. "Okay, it's all you."

Fynn hands Beans the broken bottle. "If you're

going first, then take this. It's a better weapon than that stick you're holding."

Fynn and Beans swap weapons, and I glance at Scarlett to see her hovering close to Edge.

"Ready?" Beans repeats, and we all nod.

"Stay," Edge tells Hoppy.

Down the steps the six of us slowly go. Beans, me, Rocky, Fynn, and Scarlett, with Edge bringing up the rear.

One by one we flip on the flashlights we have left as we descend the damp wooden steps into the darkness.

"The rain must have come in through the hole," Beans says, and no one responds. Like me, I think they're all more concerned with aliens right now than wet steps.

The temperature drops, and dust floats in Beans's light beam as he scans the dirt walls lining the narrow passage. Reaching forward, I grip the back of his shirt, and I barely breathe or blink as my gaze bounces around the darkness. Behind me, Rocky moves in close, and I'm happy to be sandwiched between the two of them.

Down, down, down we go, until we're standing in a room about the size of my bedroom. The floor's a little wet, just like the stairs. Shelves line the walls with cans of food and jars of jams, everything covered in dust.

"I wonder how long this has been here," Beans says.

None of us move as our lights play off the details of the small room, and I pay particular attention to the dark corners, where little bug-eyed aliens might be hiding.

But there's no one here except us. Whatever made the hole in the door was probably just another one of those silver balls.

Gradually, we begin to move away from one another to explore the small room. I pick up one of the metal cans of food and flip it over to see a date stamp: June 1932. Wow, this is old. I think about our Tennessee history unit in school this year and all the black-and-white pictures we saw of farmers and miners during the early nineteen hundreds. We also watched a black-and-white documentary about the Depression. This metal can and probably everything else in here is from that time period.

Learning about history is one thing, but actually seeing it in real life...it's almost like seeing a ghost or something.

"Check this out," Rocky says, shuffling something around, and I turn to see him pulling a chest out from the corner and into the beam of sunlight shining in from above.

He lifts the lid. Clothes lie in neatly folded piles, some men's, some women's, and others children's. Rocky picks a few pieces up and holds them out. One of the shirts looks like an old military uniform.

Fynn grabs a bar of soap wrapped in brown paper and smiles. "If anybody finds water, tell me."

Scarlett lifts out a child's romper with little buttons and ruffles. "Awww."

I hear a clank from behind me and glance over my shoulder to see Beans rifling through a canister of old junk: a watch on a chain, a tiny mirror, a small picture frame, a silver brush, a baby's rattle, and some of those knitting needles like my mom uses.

Beans shines his light around the room again. "How cool is this?"

"There it is," Edge whispers.

Everything is forgotten as we turn to see the silver object that he's found wedged under a canvas bag. The orb must've fallen through the door and down the stairs, hit the ground, and rolled underneath the bag.

The object is the exact same color as the perfectly

round balls we've already found, but this one isn't perfect. It has square knobs sticking out of it with a couple inches of space in between each knob. It sort of looks like a giant jack.

Edge slips leather gloves onto each hand and gently slides the ball out from under the bag. With a small grunt, he picks up the sphere, and I hold my breath, waiting for... I'm not sure what. The thing to move? For it to open? For the other balls we have in our packs to "recognize" it? I don't know.

Beans moves in to look. "Is it heavy?"

"I'd say it's about twenty pounds," Edge says.

Twenty pounds? The other silver balls are light. What could be inside this one that's twenty pounds?

Beans shakes his head. "That's definitely not a meteor."

"I don't see how an alien can fit in that," says Scarlett. "Or the other balls we found."

Fynn lifts a finger to touch the object and Edge moves it out of his reach. "Let's get it up top and then we can all look at it."

Carefully he starts back up the steps, and we follow. I see Hoppy looking down at us, wagging his tail, and the late afternoon sun shining in behind him.

Edge stops right as he's about to climb out and

turns down to look at us. "Hey, do you guys mind getting some of that stuff? Grab a few of the food cans, and the canister you found, Beans, and maybe one of those outfits. Everything is so old. They'd be cool souvenirs."

"Isn't that stealing?" Fynn asks.

Edge laughs. "Stealing from who? Whoever built this is long gone."

I nod. "And that food says 1932. It's been a long time since anyone's been here." I turn back around and trail the others down. "Let's get a few things."

"I call dibs on that cute little romper," Scarlett says.

"Dibs on the watch on the chain," says Beans.

"I want a can of sardines," Rocky says.

I crinkle my nose. "Why do you want sardines?"

"It's a cool can. Did you see it?" He snatches it off the shelf and turns it around. "See, it's got a pin like a key you spin to open it."

Suddenly, I hear a creaking sound behind me.

The sunlight filtering down the steps gets narrower and narrower. I look straight up to see Edge closing the rusted door to the outside.

What the . . . ?

I scramble up the steps right as he closes the door

all the way and latches it. My heart stops for a startled second before kicking in again.

"What are you doing?" I holler.

But Edge doesn't answer.

I bang on the door. "Edge! If this is a joke, it's not funny."

He doesn't answer, and with each second, panic builds within me. He can't just leave us in here! What is he doing? Through the hole in the center of the door, I see his shadow as he moves across the small clearing. He seems to be heading into the woods.

My panic morphs into full-on terror. "Edge!" I bellow.

Hoppy barks.

Rocky yells.

My terror mutates into rage. *"Edge!"*

Fynn wheezes.

Scarlett screams.

Beans dry heaves.

"EDGE!" I shriek so loudly my vocal cords hurt.

And then the batteries in our flashlight die, and we are cast into darkness.

CHAPTER 22

"He double-crossed us!" Rocky yells.

With a grunt, I push against the door, and tears swarm my eyes. "Please don't leave us in here," I say through the hole.

Silence.

"Please." My voice breaks, and the sound of it cracking irritates me. I don't want to cry. But what are we going to do? Edge can't just leave us here.

I put my arm through the hole and frantically feel around, trying to find the latch on the outside, but all I can feel is rusted metal. My arm's too short.

With a helpless sigh, I sink down onto one of the steps and rub my hands into my eyes. *It's going to be okay*, I tell myself. We'll figure this out.

Fynn's still wheezing and I glance down into the dark. "Someone get Fynn his inhaler!" Sheesh, can they not hear him? I swear, if it weren't for me, Fynn would never get his meds.

Some scrambling. A squirt. And Fynn stops gasping for air.

Scarlett fumbles up the steps toward me. The sunlight filtering through the hole hits her terrified face. She's afraid of the dark. Not only are we locked in here but when the sun goes down it's going to be completely black. She's going to freak.

She's breathing heavily, almost like she's trying not to panic but can't help it. It would really stink to be afraid of the dark. I reach down and squeeze her shoulder to try to give some assurance.

We had three flashlights. Edge had one, leaving us with the other two. "Beans, was that your light that died?"

"Yes."

"I have the one I think you were carrying," Rocky says as he flips it on and then it immediately dies. He slaps it against his palm. Slaps it again. "Uh, make that no."

Nobody says anything for a few seconds and I try

again, putting my face up to the hole in the door. "Edge, please. You can't just leave us down here."

Silence.

I can't believe I thought Edge was cute.

"What are we going to do?" Scarlett whispers.

"Help!" I yell up through the hole. "Help! Anybody?"

Silence.

Just a frog or two answers back.

I glance down into the dark. But no one says anything.

"So, um, this one time I was stuck in a car." Scarlett begins another one of her tales. "It was the coldest winter in Chicago..."

She said she embellishes for the attention, and I want to remind her she doesn't need lies for us to like her because we're okay with her now. But I have a feeling this tale is more about nerves than anything else.

"...and the lock was stuck. I banged on the window but no one heard me. Mom was in the grocery for over an hour, and when she came out, I had frostbite on my pinky toe." She looks up at me. "Swear to God."

I don't know what to say to all of that so I decide to change the subject in hopes of alleviating everyone's nerves. "Me and Beans found one of those silver balls," I announce, even though Beans wanted to keep it between him and me. But that was back when he was keeping his other secret, too, and now that everything is out in the open, I have a feeling he'll be okay with me sharing this.

"Really?" I hear Fynn say from the dark. "When?"

"Back when we were in the sugarcane field," Beans answers, not sounding annoyed that I just told the others.

"We tried to break it open, but we couldn't. We also thought it might be a bomb."

"A bomb?" Scarlett gasps. "Is it in here with us right now?"

Beans heaves a sigh. "Yes, but I'm pretty sure it's not a bomb." He shuffles up the narrow steps and sits beside us, carrying the canister with all the old supplies. "Let's just focus on getting out of here."

"Good idea," I say, and watch him rifle through the junk.

"At least we won't starve," Rocky says. "There's food down here."

"The food is fifty years old," Fynn grumbles.

Tears prick my eyes again and I blink them away. All the things we've made it through on this adventure, and now we're going to end up stuck in a cellar. "I'm sorry. I'm so sorry I ever suggested we go on this stupid trip."

"It's okay, Annie," Fynn says. "We all wanted to. It wasn't just you."

Scarlett touches my arm, and I look down to see her holding out my pocketknife. "Will this help?" she quietly asks.

"My pocketknife!" I snatch it up. "Where did you find it?"

She doesn't answer, and I get the distinct impression that she's trying to decide if she should tell the truth or not. She glances away then and mumbles so softly that I barely hear her. "I found it when we were at the Masons', grabbing stuff before we ran."

I narrow my eyes. "You've had it this whole time?"

She cringes.

"Why? You knew how important this was to me."

Scarlett ducks her head, like she's too ashamed to even look at me. "I'm sorry."

"But why?"

She shrugs.

"Scarlett, I don't understand."

"I-I was jealous of you. It was stupid." She ducks her head even lower. "I'm really sorry. I promise not to do anything like that again. I meant to give it back earlier, but I forgot."

I stare at the side of her cheek as she guiltily looks down at her fingers, and all I can think is, *She's* been jealous of *me*? Well, I guess I've been jealous of her, too, with the Rocky thing, and Edge, too, a little. So really I can't be mad. Plus, she did say that she meant to give back the pocketknife earlier. It's not like she was going to go back to Chicago with it.

"Hey," I whisper, and she drags her eyes up to look at me. "Truce, okay? Friends. Real friends."

Slowly, her face splits into this big grin, and she crawls one step up to throw her arms around my neck. "Thank you."

I'm probably taking it too far, but I'm feeling all kinds of gushy, so I say, "I'm glad we met. I'm glad to have a new friend."

Still looking through the canister, Beans snorts. "Girls."

Scarlett and I laugh, and holding my pocketknife, I get this surge of power, and it seems like a motivational speech is appropriate. "Listen, y'all. This isn't over yet. We are going to get out of here, we're going to get that thing back from Edge, and we're going to save Beans's house!"

"And then we're going home," Scarlett chimes in.

"Yes!" I say, smiling at her. "Then we're going home."

I hear one single clap from down below and stick my tongue out at whoever—Fynn or Rocky—did it, and then I hand Beans my pocketknife and scoot out of his way. "Use that if you can."

He thinks about everything for a second, and I watch as he clicks my knife open. Using some twine from the canister, he ties my knife to a metal rod. "I think this is going to be the perfect length." He hands me a small antique mirror. "You're going to be my eyes. Just give me directions."

"What are you, part of the A team?" I say, and Beans smiles.

We switch spots, and I hold the mirror out of the hole and point it at the latch. He sticks the tied contraption out, too, and starts fiddling with the latch.

Carefully, I watch. "Okay, good. Right...little left. Down..."

The tip of the blade catches on the latch, and it shakes a little as Beans concentrates. It lifts a tiny bit and I hold my breath, but Beans loses hold and the blade slips.

"Crap," Beans grumbles.

I nod. "You got this. Let's do it again." I watch through the mirror as the tip of the blade begins to near the latch again. "Left...up...*there*. Careful."

The tip dips down under the latch and this time Beans isn't slow—he flicks the blade fast and hard. The latch clicks and I shout, "You got it!"

I shove the door wide open, scrambling out, and Beans follows. We both roll to our backs, gulping in fresh air.

Scarlett flops down beside me, dramatically kissing the ground. "Oh, Lord Jesus, thank you!"

Rocky and Fynn climb out last, whooping and hollering. I smile at their silliness, glad they're good friends again. Glad the *Scouts* are good again.

With another deep breath, I start to sit up when I notice both Fynn and Rocky now silent and staring into the woods.

I follow their line of sight to see Mary Jo and Otis,

and behind those two stand all three of their boys. Fynn's arms and hands shoot straight up into the air, and the rest of us hurry to follow his lead.

Mary Jo takes a step toward us, shotgun in hand. "Well, lookee what we have 'ere."

CHAPTER 23

Otis spits a long stream of brown juice. "Yep, lookee."

Scarlett starts crying, and I don't mean a tiny little cry. I don't mean the kind that slowly builds, either. I'm talking, she goes from zero to full-on blubbery sobbing in less than a second.

I totally expect Fynn's wheezing and Beans's dry heaves next, but they both stay just like me — wide-eyed, hands in the air, staring right at the Masons.

"What were y'all doing down there?" Mary Jo asks sharply, nodding at the storm shelter door.

Scarlett inhales a choppy breath. "Th-there was this thing...th-that fell from the sky...a-and we traced it to here...and th-then Edge shut us in... b-but the cave and the rain and the field and the river and the silver balls and the skeleton." Scarlett crumples with her sobs. "P-please don't hurt us."

I've seen people on TV have panic attacks, and I think Scarlett might be having one. Carefully, with my eyes on the gun, I slide my hand to her shoulder and pat it. The gesture must work, because her sobbing quiets a little.

Otis runs his eyes over all of us. "Where be the other one? The older one?"

Pointing in the direction I saw Edge's shadow move, I don't feel one bit guilty when I say, "He went that way."

Another shotgun in hand, Otis takes off in that direction and one of their boys goes with him. Junior and the other boy stay with Mary Jo, one off to either side.

"Don't hurt Hoppy!" I yell after Otis.

"Quiet," Mary Jo barks. "Junior, you get on over there a little closer to those kids and make sure they don't run. And don't you dare mess it up this time," she warns him, and with his head down, he drags his feet closer to us.

She looks around the clearing at the silver gunk and the charred grass. Then she reaches inside her dress pocket and pulls out Beans's map. "Which one of yuns is gonna tell us what ya found?"

None of us open our mouths.

But then she cocks the shotgun, and we all start babbling at once.

"Meteor shower—"

"Basinger's silo—"

"Silver dust—"

"Beans is moving—"

"Almost drowned—"

"Bats—"

"The balls—"

Mary Jo lifts the barrel toward the sky and shoots, and the boom echoes off the mountains and the valleys, the trees and the ground. We fall silent in shock. I've never actually heard a gun go off before. It's loud. And scary.

The other Mason boy snickers, and Scarlett and I both start shaking.

Mary Jo points the shotgun at Rocky. "You. Speak."

He does, quickly, stuttering and fumbling over his words, but he manages to get the entire story told.

"And none of yuns know what you found?" she asks.

We shake our heads. I wonder if Mary Jo knows what's going on.

"Okay, this is what we're doing." She trails her gun

over all of us. "Empty yer pockets, yer backpacks, whatever you have on ya. I want a pile there." She indicates a spot on the ground. "No funny business. You hear?"

We nod.

"And you." She looks right at Fynn. "Make sure you git that thingy for yer breathin' problem."

"Yes, ma'am."

We hurry and do exactly as we're told, emptying what little we have left into a pile and taking a seat on the ground.

"You." Mary Jo looks pointedly at me. "Dark-haired girl."

"Annie," I tell her, though I'm not sure why.

"Bring me that there silver thing." She gestures toward our pile, where Beans's silver ball is.

I don't hesitate. I walk over and pick up the ball. It feels warm now, different than it did before. Actually, it's more like hot, and holding it makes my hands tingle, almost like the sphere is vibrating.

"Bring it 'ere, girl."

I glance over to my friends, all huddled, staring back at me. I look up at Junior to see he's looking at me now. Then he surprises the heck out of me by giving a tiny nod toward the woods. Like he's saying, *Go*.

I whirl around and throw the ball as hard as I can in Mary Jo's direction and I yell, *"Run!"*

My friends don't hesitate to jump to their feet, and we all take off in a mad sprint toward the woods.

A shot fires and it vibrates the air around us, but we keep running at full speed straight into the trees.

"She's shooting at us!" Scarlett screams.

We tear through the woods, not looking back, running...running...running. Next to me Fynn starts really panting, and I know he'll be wheezing soon.

Scarlett's falling back. I'm not losing anybody again, so I wait until she catches up, grab her hand, and drag her behind me.

Beside me Rocky trips and rolls, and Fynn doesn't miss a beat as he ducks down, grabs Rocky's arm, and yanks him right back up.

"Thanks, bro," Rocky pants, and wheezing for air, Fynn nods.

"Over there!" Beans points to a huge fallen tree.

We all leap over the log and pile on top of one another behind it.

Fynn fumbles for his inhaler, and I try to help him with it, but Rocky beats me to it, sticking it between Fynn's lips. It's the first time I've seen Rocky do that.

After a couple of squirts, we try to be quiet and

listen, but all of us are breathing so heavily that it's not really working.

Seconds go by. Then a couple of minutes, and as I finally get my breathing completely under control, I listen carefully for any movement.

"I think we lost them," Rocky whispers, peeking over the downed tree.

"They do have what they want," Beans quietly says.

Fynn starts to get up. "Let's go before they find us."

Beans nods. "Keep quiet and low to the ground."

Just as we start to move, another shot booms in the distance, and Mary Jo calls, "Come out, come out, wherever you are. We've got your friend and his little dog, too."

Oh, no, not Hoppy! I look at everyone. "What are we going to do?" I whisper. "We can't just leave them."

Rocky scoffs. "Are you kidding me? Edge locked us down in that cellar."

True.

But as much as I despise Edge and just want to go home, the idea of leaving him and Hoppy to the Mason Clan just doesn't sit right.

I look around at the Scouts and can see the same thought running through everyone's head.

Do we help him or do we run for our lives?

CHAPTER 24

Minutes later I walk out from the woods and into the clearing. "Mary Jo, I'm here to turn myself in."

Straightening up, she turns around to survey me.

I put my hands into the air and walk closer. "Please don't hurt Edge and Hoppy."

Beans comes flying out of the woods behind me. "No, Annie!" He grabs my arm. "What are you doing?"

I try to shake Beans off. "We talked about this. Mary Jo and the rest of them are too smart. We can't outrun them. We have to turn ourselves in." I shuffle to the side, and Mary Jo's gaze follows me. "I'm sorry we gave you so many problems."

With a grunt, she looks down at Beans's plaid boxers. "Where're yer pants, boy?"

He cringes in embarrassment. "I had an accident in them."

It takes her a second to realize what he just said, and then she cackles and cackles, like it's the funniest thing in the world that a boy had an accident in his pants. What an awful woman.

I glance beyond her, surveying the clearing. Mary Jo is here with Junior and one of her other sons. Otis and the third brother must be out looking for us now. Edge and Hoppy are sitting on the ground with Junior behind them. The silver balls are over to the side in a pile. They look less silver now and more yellow. Maybe it's just a trick of the light, but something about them doesn't seem right.

Junior and his brother are focused on us. I keep my hands up. "Do you promise not to hurt my friends?"

"I ain't promising nothin'."

I shuffle a little more, and Mary Jo turns to fully face me. Beans rushes over and grabs one of my hands out of the air. "No, Annie."

He clenches my fingers tight and I feel him transfer over one end of the elasticized wire he had woven into the waistband of his jeans. Kind of like the trick vest he made last year—he had done the same thing with his pants by incorporating survival items into the waistband and the seams. That's why his jeans are high-waters.

And to think that I thought Beans's mom hadn't bought him new clothes. Their financial situation had nothing to do with why his pants didn't fit.

"You and I are sticking together," he says.

Mary Jo gives our clasped hands a quick annoyed look. "All right. Whatever. Git on over here."

Slowly, we move forward. I glance one more time behind her to see all eyes still on us. Then I fake sneeze, loudly, as our predetermined signal, and everything after that happens in a blur.

Scarlett and Fynn fly out of their hiding spot in the woods, holding an ultrastrong thin rope that had previously been the seam of Beans's pants. The two of them tackle the brother as Rocky races straight toward us.

Beans and I take off in different directions, holding the elasticized titanium wire. We circle Mary Jo, crisscrossing in the rear and swerving back around to the front. Rocky grabs the shotgun from her hand, ducks under our wire, and races across the clearing. Beans and I dart around the front of Mary Jo again, switch directions, and head to crisscross in the rear.

Mary Jo screams and hollers and thrashes, and we

do one more swerving wrap. Then we yank, hard, and she goes barreling to the ground, sending a gust of silver dust up into the air. Beans grabs my end of the wire and does a quick knot, and we both take a step back.

"I'm gonna git you kids!" She kicks and bicycles her big legs, trying to roll over, and then kicks some more.

Beans looks at me, and we both burst out laughing. She looks like one of those pigs-in-a-blanket things that my mom makes, when she takes a hot dog and wraps it in crescent dough.

Beans's plan worked perfectly. He really is brilliant. I turn and tell him just that. "Beans, you are the smartest kid I know."

He gives me an embarrassed smile that warms me down to my toes. I have the best friends ever.

"Leave my mama alone!" one of the boys yells, and we turn to see the one Fynn and Scarlett tackled and trussed up with the thin rope. He's rolling around on the ground just like his mom.

Edge stands next to Rocky now, and Junior sits on the ground, unharmed as I insisted, looking at Mary Jo and not bothering to hide his own grin.

"Junior!" Mary Jo bellows, craning her neck, trying to see around the clearing.

"Leave Junior alone," Otis says, stepping from the trees to lay his shotgun down before putting his hands into the air. "This has gone too far."

Mary Jo makes a couple of grumpy noises. "Now, you just hold on—"

"I said," Otis snaps, "this has gone too far." Then, without us telling him to do so, he walks over and sits down beside Junior.

My friends and I look at one another. I don't think any of us can believe that Otis just got all authoritative with Mary Jo, or that he's giving himself up.

"Where's the other one?" Edge asks.

"He took off," Otis says. "That one always was a coward."

Something vibrates through the air, and I look around. "What is that?" I turn to Beans. "Do you hear that?"

Nodding, he rotates in a slow circle, looking at the ground and the trees and all around. "Yeah, I hear it, too."

"Hey," Rocky calls from across the clearing. "Do you feel that?"

Feel? Yeah, he's right. Whatever it is, it's tickling the hair on my arms. I rub at them and turn to Fynn and Scarlett, who are both staring at the pile of silver balls.

Only they're definitely not silver anymore. They're dark yellow, and as I watch, they slowly transition into orange, and as I keep watching, I realize that they're vibrating.

Fynn takes a giant step back, grabbing Scarlett as he does. "Th-th-they're going to explode!"

Mary Jo squirms against the wire, and I move quickly. "Help me," I tell Beans as I'm already starting to untie her. No matter how much I don't like her, I'm not going to let her get blown up.

Something in the trees moves, and I glance up to see at least a dozen men and women dressed in camouflage step into the clearing.

My hands shoot straight up into the air because — my eyes widen — every single one of the group has a rifle.

And the rifles are pointed right at us.

CHAPTER 25

"Sit," one of them commands, and all of us immediately do.

Silently, the group of military people spreads out around the clearing to surround us. They shift the focus of their rifles off us and hold them braced in front, and I quietly expel a breath of relief. Mary Jo holding a gun to us is one thing, but the military? Yeah, so much more intimidating.

The one who commanded "Sit" points to where Beans and Mary Jo and I are. "I want all of you here. Now."

Everyone immediately moves, scurrying across the clearing to sit beside me and Beans and Mary Jo.

Two of the military guys pick up the one trussed boy and carry him over to none-too-gently drop him next to our clump.

The vibrating noise becomes louder, and I glance across to see the balls going from orange to red. Automatically, my friends and I inch closer to one another, and I feel one of them shaking.

No, wait. That's me.

Scarlett grabs my hand. I grab Beans's. And one by one, we all link fingers. "I'm sorry," I murmur, apologizing again.

Fynn slides Hoppy into his lap. "This is all of our faults."

Scarlett squeezes my hand. "We're in this together," she says, and Beans and Rocky both nod.

Tears blur across my eyes, and I sniff. My stupid friends. God, I love them.

We watch as one of the military men crouches beside the glowing spheres. He consults his watch and then presses his finger to an earpiece as he listens to whoever is on the other end. Abruptly, he stands and shouts, "Incoming!"

A gush of wind whips through the clearing then, and several of the military move in to protect our clump as a whooping noise fills the air.

"What's that?" Scarlett yells.

The whooping gets louder.

"A helicopter!" Beans yells back.

And louder still.

My black braids whip my face, and I cover my ears with my hands as I glance up to see a helicopter whirl over the tree line to hover above us.

Three people dressed in the same camo fatigues zip down to land in the clearing. As soon as their feet hit the charred grass, they unclip their zip lines, and the helicopter takes off again, tilting and whooping off across the sky.

One of the new people is carrying a hard black case, and together the three of them sprint over to the balls. As the men kneel next to the spheres and lay the case down, I look at their faces and realize the one with the case is... *Dad?*

"Dad!" I shout.

He looks over at me and holds up his hand. "Stay there, sweetie."

I look over at Beans, like he might have the answer to my silent question: *What is my dad doing here?*

Oh, my God. Does he hunt aliens? Holy cow, Dad is cool!

I watch as Dad flips the case open and spreads it

wide. Black foam lines the interior, and a ball just like the others already sits inside. It's also glowing red.

Quickly, Dad pulls on a pair of thick gloves and carefully picks up the first vibrating sphere in the pile. Fear works its way through my chest as I continue watching him. *Please be careful, Dad. Please.*

He places the sphere inside the case. Then he does the same with another and another and another, working swiftly and cautiously to cradle each within the black foam. The last one is the larger one with all the knobs. Dad rotates the ball, studying it, and then turns one of the knobs before placing the ball in the center of the case and grabbing what looks like a remote. He points it at the case and presses some buttons, and the spheres go from vibrating to full-on shaking.

One of the military guys kneeling beside him stands up and backs away, and I watch as Dad points the remote at the case and punches more buttons.

The spheres get redder. And redder. And redder still, and the guy who backed away casts a nervous look around the clearing.

The color of the balls shifts again, going from red back to orange, from orange to yellow, from yellow to white. And then the spheres begin glowing brighter. And brighter. And so bright now, I have to squint to keep looking, like looking into the sun.

"That's not normal," I hear one of the military people whisper.

I clench Scarlett's fingers and Beans clenches mine.

Feverishly, Dad jabs at more buttons. "It's too late!"

"Did he turn the right knob?" I hear someone else ask at the exact second Dad yells, "Cover!"

Every single military person standing around throws their body on top of us. Through the gaps in the arms and legs, I watch as lasers zing from the orbs, connecting them all, glowing so brightly that it hurts to look. I feel the intensity on my face as the radiance heats my skin.

Two people race toward Dad, and they are carrying a metal box. Dad closes the lid on the black case, and the bright light dims to a glow that I can see through the seams. Carefully, he lifts and places the case in the metal box before locking that lid, and then he and the other two people leave everything there and take off sprinting across the clearing right toward us.

Boom!

The metal box lifts about a foot off the ground and silver dust shoots out of its seams. Then the box falls back down to the dirt and starts popping around as the spheres punch out from the inside, leaving huge dents in the box.

But just as quickly as it went off, the box comes to a sudden stop.

Panting, I gaze out from under all the people, searching for my dad. He's right here. On top of our body pile.

Slowly, everyone begins crawling off, and after that, Scarlett's shaking is the first thing I notice.

Then Fynn's breathing. Heavy, but not wheezing.

Beans's death grip on my arm comes to me third.

Rocky's heartbeat filters in last, and I realize he's pressed up against me. Protecting me.

All of us, actually, are squished together, protecting one another. Me and the Scouts, with Hoppy in the middle of us all.

I blink a few times but see only dots, blink a few more times, and my vision slowly returns. I look for Dad again, and he's already back across the clearing near the metal box, talking to several of the military people.

We're alive. We're alive!

Everyone moves around, beginning to clean up, and Dad crosses the charred grass back our way. I don't waste a second jumping up and running into his arms.

"Dad," I sob into his shoulder. "I'm sorry. I'm so sorry."

He doesn't say anything, just squeezes me tight, and I think it has to be about the best hug he's ever given me.

Dad finally lets go. "You, my dear, are in a lot of trouble." He casts a disciplinary look over my friends. "All of you are."

Yeah, I saw that coming.

Two of the military people cut Mary Jo and her son from their restraints, and once she's on her feet again, she turns a snarly look onto my dad. "Where's our money?" she demands.

Dad shakes his head. "We don't pay for misinformation."

Scarlett jabs her finger in the Masons' direction. "They kidnapped us and locked us in a shed!"

"Oh, we didn't hurt 'em." Mary Jo waves off Scarlett's accusation. "We was just trying to keep 'em in one place like you said. We called ya, didn't we?"

Me and my friends all look at each other. *What is she talking about?*

Dad turns to Otis and merely lifts his brows, clearly wanting an explanation.

Otis casts a guilty look to the ground. "Things did get a little out of hand, but we didn't hurt 'em. Scared 'em, sure. Every kid needs a good lesson every now 'n' then."

"Your job," my dad says, "was to keep them in one place if you found them, and to consult on the terrain."

Otis gives a little shrug. "Sorry," he mumbles.

Dad folds his arms and looks between Otis and Mary Jo, and then he turns and looks at all of us. "Did they hurt you?"

Reluctantly, we all shrug and shake our heads because the truth is, the Masons didn't actually hurt us. Just scared us real good.

"See," Mary Jo says. "They's fine. And I bet they did learn a lesson with all their lying and snooping." She straightens up. "Thanks to us."

"Okay, so we did lie and snoop," I grudgingly admit. "But it's not your job to teach us a lesson. You really did scare us."

In response, Mary Jo just snorts.

"B-b-but what about Old Man Basinger?" Scarlett stammers. "We think they might have killed him."

Mary Jo scrunches up her face. "We ain't never killed nobody. And I saw Basinger just the other day."

"But you have his shotgun in your shed," Scarlett says.

Mary Jo scoffs. "I've had that thing for over a decade. Basinger gave it to us in exchange for some moonshine."

"Then whose skeleton was that?" I ask.

Dad holds his hand up. "It's true, Mr. Basinger is alive and well. What skeleton are you talking about?"

"In the cave, Dad. There was a skeleton, and it was wearing a hat with Old Man Basinger's name in it."

Edge bursts out laughing. "I can't believe you guys fell for that fake bag of bones. I wish I could've been there when you found it. Did you scream?" He laughs some more. "I bought that at a Halloween shop a couple of years ago. I was actually hoping one of my cousins would find it." He slaps his leg and hoots some more.

I scowl at him, and Scarlett steps right up and kicks him in the shin.

"Ow!" Edge jumps back, and I smirk.

Rocky narrows his eyes. "You were hanging near the cave, waiting to see if someone found it, weren't you?"

Edge shrugs. "Sort of. I was actually out looking for the meteor when I ran into you all."

"That's the only reason why you teamed up with us. Why you were nice to us." Beans peels his lips off his braces. "You knew we were your best bet at finding it."

Dad gives Edge a good long study. "You're one of the Basingers, aren't you?"

"What?" My jaw drops. "You never said that!"

Edge shrugs again. "Harmless omission."

I turn to my dad. "He locked us in that shelter. And he was going to steal—"

"I was going to let you out," Edge says. "Or at minimum tell someone where you all were."

My jaw drops again. "What, after you kept everything for yourself? You're awful!"

Dad motions a military guy over. "One of my team will give you a ride home. I'll be talking to your parents and your grandfather tomorrow."

Edge's cockiness disappears, and I grin. Good. He deserves whatever he gets for being so mean. And to think I thought he was cute.

Dad nods to the Mason Clan. "My team will escort you home, too."

Mary Jo casts one last growly look our way, before heading off.

"Junior," I call, and he turns around. "Thank you again."

He gives a little smile and nod, and I watch as he jogs across the grass and ducks between two trees.

With his arms folded, Dad turns and looks at all of us. "Now, for you all. The fort. The tree house. The basement. All the little notes you left. There will be no more of that. There will also be no more camping trips. I can't speak for your parents, but I will say Annie's grounded for the whole summer."

I hang my head. That's a long time.

There's silence for a moment as the punishment sinks in.

Scarlett nudges me and whispers, "Your dad is pretty great."

I nod. He is. This whole thing—this is why Dad kept telling me to stay at Rocky's. He knew something might happen with the meteor shower.

"Are you a spy, Dad?" Because I always thought he was an accountant.

"I work for the Department of Defense," he says.

"What you saw was a top secret project. It was being tested during the meteor shower, and obviously several things went wrong."

"So they were bombs?" Beans asks.

"They weren't supposed to be, but it was turning into that," Dad says. "The red, the vibrating. The closer the components came to each other, the more they reacted. I don't think you kids realize how close we came to an explosion."

We all exchange a surprised look. Thank God the military showed up.

"Then what were they supposed to be?" Rocky asks.

Dad smiles a little. "Without giving great detail, it was a spy satellite system we were testing."

"Wow," Beans whispers. "What were you spying on?"

"Mmm, a few things in the area," Dad cryptically says, with an involuntary glance in the direction of the caves. A spark of curiosity has me exchanging silent looks with my friends.

"No." Dad points at all of us. "Get those looks off your faces. Like I said, we were testing the satellite system, and if all went well, we planned to use it for other classified things. However, as you saw, things didn't go as planned."

"What about the silvery stuff that was everywhere?" Scarlett asks.

"Yeah," Fynn says, looking down at some of it stuck to his arm. "We're not infected, are we?"

Dad chuckles. "No. Best way I can explain the silver dust is that it's like exhaust. It spewed out of the balls as they tracked through the sky. It will not harm you, don't worry." Dad motions toward his team working all around us. "By the time they're done cleaning, it'll be like none of this even happened."

"What about the Masons?" I ask. "It seemed like you knew them."

"Actually, Mr. Mason helped us five years ago with some mapping of the caves. When we were having difficulties obtaining signals from the project this time around, we asked him to assist in the ground search. It was about that time that I realized you kids were gone, and I asked him to keep an eye out for you as well."

Dad makes eye contact with each of us. "I deal with some pretty scary things in my job, but nothing has ever been as terrifying as thinking about you kids out here in the hills by yourselves. You will never scare me like that again. Do you understand?"

We nod.

I glance over at Beans, and it hits me what this all really means. There is no crashed meteor. No money. Beans is leaving.

I grasp his arm. "We can still figure it out," I tell him, and my brain scrambles for a new plan—anything that'll stop my best friend from leaving.

With a sad smile, he shakes his head. He's given up. But I don't accept that. We can still figure something out, can't we? We have to!

But even as my mind races, the reality of the whole situation sinks in. One of my best friends is moving, and no amount of plotting or strategy is going to change that. It's out of my hands.

We're just going to have to figure out how to see each other even though we'll be an hour apart. Because there's no way I'm saying goodbye to Beans.

Eventually, the place is cleaned up and Dad leads us away, along with the rest of his team. But it's only when we're away from the clearing and back in the woods that I remember the metal box. The military people never did take it.

Pausing for a second, I glance over my shoulder, through the trees and back into the clearing, and my hands fly to my mouth. There by the box, looking down at it with egg-shaped eyes, stands a tall thing with long arms and legs, a small head, and skin that seems both speckled with green and also see-through at the same time.

I blink hard, not even sure if I'm actually seeing the creature or not. But as quick as it's there, it's gone.

CHAPTER 26

Sunlight flickers across my lids, and slowly, I open them. It's Saturday morning and I'm supposed to help Mom clean the house.

Ugh.

But I do have my last swimming lesson today and I'm excited. I get a certificate and everything. I can dive now. And hold my breath under water for almost a minute. I can swim freestyle for five whole laps without stopping.

I mean, I'm not going to go and join the swim team or anything, but at least now I don't freak out at the thought of water. And I made some new friends. In fact, tomorrow they're all coming over to my house to watch a movie and eat pizza.

With a stretch and a yawn, I lie here for a second thinking about Monday. The first day of seventh grade. Summer's been good (even with being grounded), but I'm definitely ready for school to start. Mom offered to drive me, Fynn, and Rocky as a first-day-of-school treat, but they both said no. Rocky's riding with some of his football friends, and Fynn's riding with his girlfriend.

That's right—his girlfriend.

They met at Vacation Bible School and she lives on the other side of town. Her family just moved here from Kentucky. Every time she sees me and Fynn hanging out, she gets all mean, grabbing his hand and holding it so tight I swear his fingers are going to fall off. But Fynn still hangs out with just me and Rocky all the time, so I really don't care.

Anyway, I promised Junior I'd ride the bus with him on the first day. Dad did some calling around, and even though the other two Mason boys are being "homeschooled" by Mary Jo, Junior stood up to her and insisted on attending a real school. So he and I are going to sit next to each other on the bus, and I'm excited about it.

My walkie crackles. "Annie, it's Rocky. Over."

With a grin, I pick it up. "This is Annie. Over."

"Beans is going to be here tonight. Over."

I sit straight up in bed, excitement bouncing all around inside me. "I know. Can't wait! Over."

"Be at my place at eight tonight. Over."

"I'll bring Pringles. Over."

Setting my walkie down, I bounce out of bed and nearly skip through all of my chores. This is the first time we're all going to hang out together since our adventure. I can't wait to see Beans. He still had to move, but we talk on the phone all the time, and he seems happier at his dad's house. I'm glad for him, even though I miss him like crazy.

That evening, Dad points his finger at me as I'm heading out the door. "Do *not* go on Basinger's property."

"I won't. I promise." There's no way I'm going to risk being grounded again.

"I fully intend on calling Rocky's father to check up on you multiple times," he says.

I laugh. "Okay, Dad. I promise."

Mom waves me off. "Have fun. Be back by ten."

I jump on my BMX and race over to Rocky's. I take the rope ladder all the way up to the tree house.

Fynn, Rocky, and Beans are already here. I'm so

happy Fynn didn't bring his girlfriend. He's been pretty cool about that when there's Scouts stuff going on.

There's a pizza box sitting in the middle of the tree house, a real telescope set up next to the window, a cooler full of RC Colas, and some of Fynn's home-made brownies with what look like coconut shavings on top.

Ducking under the overhang, I plop down beside Beans and toss the chips I brought into the center. I give Beans a hug. "Missed you."

"Me, too." He gives me another look. "Hey, are you wearing lipstick?"

"It's lip gloss, thank you very much. Scarlett gave it to me for my birthday." I straighten up, daring any of them to say anything.

Rocky smiles, and it zings all kinds of butterflies through me. "Well, what do you know? Annie's a girl."

I nod. "Yes, I am. I may even wear a dress and a bow on Monday," I say, even though there is no way I'd ever wear a bow. A dress maybe, but never a bow.

Laughing, Fynn offers me hand sanitizer, and I shake my head as I reach for a slice of pizza.

Fynn asks, "Did Scarlett tell you she's coming for Christmas break?"

"Yes!" I say. "I can't wait."

Rocky plops a pepperoni into his mouth. "Christmas break, you say?"

As usual, like with Rocky and Scarlett stuff, a little bit of jealousy sparks in me. I honestly don't know if Rocky is still crushing on her. He never talks about her, and all Scarlett talks about is some older boy she likes.

Sometimes I wish everything could go back to the way it was before I started liking Rocky, and Fynn got a girlfriend, and Beans moved. But some of the changes have been pretty great. Like becoming friends with Junior and Scarlett, doing things with my new swim lesson pals, and also the whole maybe-being-brothers thing between Rocky and Fynn. Their parents are still dating, and believe it or not, they're already talking marriage. Seems soon to me, but whatever. They seem to really love each other. More importantly, though, Rocky is excited about the idea of being stepbrothers with Fynn.

But back to Scarlett. I never would've guessed, but she and I have turned into good friends. We talk on the phone at least once a week, and we've even gotten into the pen pal thing.

"I saw Edge at the Dairy Queen last week," Fynn says. "I flipped him off."

We all laugh.

I tell them, "And I saw him out working in Old Man Basinger's field. He did not look happy. I think he got in worse trouble than we did."

Beans reaches into his backpack and pulls out a copy of *National Enquirer* magazine. He opens it up to a dog-eared page. "You guys seen this?"

There's a grainy picture of a tall, long-limbed thing, with a small head and big oval eyes. In the bottom right-hand corner is a photo of Mary Jo with a headline that reads:

MY ABDUCTION BY AN ALIEN!

I've thought about that creature in the clearing, wondering if I actually saw an alien or not. I even asked my dad about it, and he just laughed it off. I couldn't tell if he was faking or not.

I don't know, and I'm not sure I ever will. But for the hundredth time since that weekend, I tell my friends, "I told you I saw something standing in the clearing as we were walking away."

I wait for them to roll their eyes or laugh, like they have every other time I've said it this summer, but this time they don't give me that reaction. This time I think they might believe me.

Taking a bite of pizza, I chew and swallow, thinking specifically about that afternoon in the clearing with the silver balls. "So, um, you guys ever think about that spy satellite system? I know Dad said they were testing it, but why this area? What do you think they were really looking for? Do you think there's something hidden in one of the caves?"

I look at Rocky, Rocky looks at Fynn, Fynn looks at Beans, and then they all three look right at me. Though no one says it out loud, and it's against all our parents' rules and restrictions, I know they're all thinking what I am:

Time for another Scouts adventure!

AUTHOR'S NOTE

I grew up in East Tennessee with family and friends who made my childhood amazing. Every day was an adventure...and if there wasn't something to explore, we invented it!

All around us were mountains, valleys, woods, creeks, whitewater rapids, caves, and the occasional wild animal. There was also the lore of the land, like the ongoing rumor of the clan who lived deep in the forest and captured kids. (Of course, this wasn't a real thing!) In *Scouts*, Annie and her friends embark on a grand escapade in which they encounter many of the same things I did as a child, including the cave, the rapids, the silo, lighting carpet on fire, the old farmer with the shotgun, and so much more.

I have a deep love and respect for the south and am so blessed to have grown up there. I hope you got a thrill out of this story as much as I enjoyed writing it and reliving my whimsical childhood.

XO,
Shannon

ACKNOWLEDGMENTS

To my lovely and energetic agent, Gemma Cooper, who fell in love with Annie's voice within the first paragraph of reading her. Thank you, Gemma, for encouraging me to write Annie's story and for working so hard to bring her to life!

To my amazing and hardworking team at JIMMY Patterson Books: Jenny Bak, Sasha Henriques, Tracy Shaw, Linda Arends, Sabrina Benun, Erinn McGrath, and Julie Guacci. You have made this such a fun and rewarding experience for me!

And to James Patterson, who wrote the foreword to *Scouts:* It is a true honor to have support from such a talented and successful author!

ABOUT THE AUTHOR

SHANNON GREENLAND grew up in Tennessee, where she dreaded all things reading and writing. She didn't even read her first book for enjoyment until she was twenty-five. After that, she was hooked! When she's not writing, she works as an adjunct math professor and lives on the coast in Florida with her very grouchy dog.